The Woodsmen

Chris Glode

First published by Dog Ear Publishing
4010 W. 86th Street, Ste H
Indianapolis, IN 46268
www.dogearpublishing.net

dog ear
PUBLISHING

ISBN: 978-159858-774-6

This book is printed on acid-free paper.

This book is a work of Fiction. Places, events, and situations in this book are purely
Fictional and any resemblance to actual persons, living or dead, is coincidental.

Printed in the United States of America

Dedicated to the lost town of Valsetz; my great-great-uncle, Joe Glode, who logged the great spruce in the Coast Range for the Army; and to all the men and women who work in the woods.

This book is a work of fiction, and no characters or events were based on actual events.

There were not too many photos of Boone, but the aging father looked at his favorite one. It was the two of them splitting firewood. Boone was just a little boy at the time.

Robert found himself sitting in his chair and staring at the photo as the afternoon sun began its descent to the west. He could smell the bourbon on his breath, but the taste was not the reason for his tears. He could remember that day when he handed the kid the splitting maul. Boone could barely pick it up. His mother yelled from the kitchen, telling Robert not to let him swing the maul. Nevertheless he did, over and over again without much success, often coming close to splitting his own leg, let alone the logs. Being the youngest, he was always asking questions and needing attention, even up until the day he died.

As Robert held his father's pistol, a lump began to grow in his throat. The gun felt good in his hand, an original Colt .45. It was the only thing he kept clean in the house, and was about the only meaningful item his father left behind. He chuckled momentarily, looking at the gun, knowing that he could not do it, but the thought often crossed his mind. No less since the accident either.

Lifting his head, he glanced over the house. Many of the family photos were hanging crookedly on the walls. Some of the frames were broken in late night frustrations, sparked by anger and all-day drunks. Many of the pictures were fading with age and dust. Only Billy was around the house now, and no one had bothered to clean or care for the place in months.

The stove did not seem to be getting any warmer. He had tried to start a fire an hour ago, but it must not have taken. He shook his head again in frustration and began to take another sip of drink. *No need*, he thought, *be heading toward the bar soon enough*. Pointing the gun with his good hand, he aimed across the living room at a beer bottle. His finger nudged at the trigger, his arm swaying in the still air.

"Has it come down to this?" he asked himself, thinking how he'd buried his wife and his boy in the same month.

He whispered, "I'm trying, Mary. I'm trying really hard." His arm was beginning to get tired holding the gun. He lowered it, took another sip, coughing violently afterward. He set the gun down on the table and began to lift himself up. Taking one last look at the picture, he tossed it on the couch and began to walk toward the front deck. He passed by a mirror resting on the wall near the front door, catching a quick glance at his weathered face. His face was numb by whiskey, chest sore from sadness. The sun was still shining through the tall trees. Shadows appeared, signaling that evening was trying to make its return. Robert felt for his keys and started his truck. Wiping the tears away, he reached for his can of chew.

He mumbled, "Wonder how Billy is doing?"

1

The sweat poured off his face as his chainsaw began its back cut, digging the dawgs into the rear of the tree, watching as the chain began to make its cut. The tall fir tree began to lean and dance around a little in the afternoon breeze. Billy grabbed a wedge out of his pocket and began hammering it, watching as the tree slowly began to separate itself. His arms did not respond as they had earlier in the day. Each swing was more tiresome than the one before. *Fall the hell over*, he thought, sweat now dripping down his chest. The tree began to show itself; each thrust against the wedge exposed the cut. Billy heard a pop, glanced to the side of the tree, and watched as it landed hard along the bushy slope.

He paused momentarily to look at his earlier work. This was Billy's fifth tank of gas and his day was coming to an end. His chain was dull, his bar had a slight bend, and his head was still heavy from the night before. Brief moments of clarity would come and go throughout the day, but for the most part he was moving slower than usual. He set the saw down between his legs and rested his arms on the bar. The only sound he heard was his breathing. No other saws were running—nothing—just his lungs begging for a good breath.

It had been a warm spring day, and the early evening sun began to show its slow decline over the western ridgeline. Patches of morning dew still remained where the tall shadows once stood. Fallen timber and saw chips created a new forest floor, and the eastern slope was now covered in downed trees and wooded tomb-stones. With a few decent fallers, these hillsides could be transformed in a matter of hours, and today was no exception. In the distance, the last whistle punk sounded, signaling the shift coming to an end. Back to town, another Friday night at the tavern.

"I'm buying the first round," Billy said as he threw his chainsaw and pack into the bed of the Ford truck. His boots were caked in mud and sawdust, and his hickory shirt was soaked in sweat and dirt from the past week's work.

"About time," Red said in a delayed response. The aging man then limped toward the passenger seat where the family golden retriever greeted him. Billy fired up the truck and they began to drive down to the rest of the crew.

"I'll see you boys in town," Billy yelled from the driver's seat. His brakes screeched as he momentarily stopped to watch the loader load its last tree of the day. The sounds of the machine did not sit well with Billy, even months after the accident. Most of the crew had already turned off their equipment and were waiting for word the shift was over.

The Ford began its long, winding trek back into town, weaving its way through the gravesites of second growth timber. Small hillsides and canyons were exposed, allowing the two men to view the foothills of the Oregon Coast Range. Neither Billy nor Red had much to say on the trip back in. Red had closed his eyes, as Billy began to ponder.

One logging road led to another before they approached the last gravel road into their hometown of Hemlock. Billy always loved the end of his shift, because it allowed a moment of clarity in between work and drink. This brief moment gave Billy the chance to gather his thoughts. It was a time when he could stop thinking about logging or his family's miseries. It allowed him to flee his normal habits and drift someplace else.

Images of his younger brother drifted in and out of his mind when he felt a slight bump. The truck had found pavement. A couple of the younger guys from the crew were trying to get around Billy. Looking in the rearview mirror, he could see them smiling and flipping him off. Billy pushed his foot to the floor and the truck quickly began to accelerate. Red was now wide awake and sitting up in his seat. The retriever mindlessly lay between the two men, only lifting its eyes in response to the speed.

Billy was rather quiet and shy, until he drank, which helped him to speak louder and more freely. He had always spoken more with actions rather than words. In high school he was a very good football player and had briefly gone off to the state college to play. He enjoyed sports and at times was rather competitive. But sitting in classes and staring off into the distant forests made his stay in college rather short. He left school and sports behind. He felt more at ease in the woods; it took less effort. Growing up with three brothers, he was always a better athlete than the other two. Whatever he seemed to do, he did it well, whether football or logging, drinking or talking shop. The glory days were long gone, as he was beginning to age rather quickly, even though only in his late 20's. His knees and back were beginning to ache more from the countless hours of hiking through the woods and running saw.

Red joked and said, "Better hit it hard around this turn or they will getcha."

"No way," Billy responded, placing two hands on the wheel. The turns ended and a half-mile straightaway stood between them and the local tavern. Billy again planted his foot to the floorboard and sent the Ford hustling down the road. The crew behind him shot into the other lane and began to accelerate. Their truck was slightly newer and it began to make ground. The rural homes of Hemlock flew by as the trucks aimed ahead. Red briefly took his eye off the road to watch the older homes, rundown barns, and overgrown lawns quickly come and go. Billy noticed his truck was losing ground and within a few seconds, the boys flew by yelling out the window. Billy relented and eased on the gas as they entered the downtown area of Hemlock. The fire station, hardware store, and grocery store crowded the main street. The tavern sat at the edge of town and Billy turned the Ford to the parking lot, where he saw the faster truck waiting.

The two choker boys in the truck got out and stood tall and proud, grinning as if they had just gotten laid for the first time.

"Fuck you guys," Billy said, shaking his head. The rival racers exchanged handshakes and friendly punches.

One of the boys responded, "You must be getting old, Billy, giving up just like that. It's sad to see."

Billy turned back to his truck and made sure the window was down for the dog. The dog briefly lifted his head in an attempt for some attention. Billy ran his hand across the top of the dog's head a few times. Red was laughing to himself as he walked into the bar. Billy noticed his father's truck in the parking lot, and then quickly scanned the main street of town.

Hemlock was originally a logging camp along the eastern side of the coast range foothills. Parts of town had not changed much since it was settled a hundred years before, when early arrivals attempted to farm the area. Half the homes in town were built in its beginning. The spring rains recently created several different shades of green across the rolling hills and distant woody canyons.

The town had slowly developed into a small community that supported the loggers. Over time, it molded itself as the middle ground between the valley, cities and the mill town of Cadillac. The logging heyday had come and gone, and now the town population supported all types. Billy glanced down the guts of town long enough to hear its silence, long enough to grab his can of chew and take a dip. Smoke was rising from the chimneys in town, scattered between the oak and fir trees, the brick and wooded buildings. Just a few hundred folks lived in Hemlock, and it did not take long, even on a Friday night, to clear out. Sounds began to erupt from inside Ray's place. At times, the tavern would get a little rowdy.

2

"How did it go today, son?" Robert asked as he ignored his drinking partner momentarily to show attention toward his boy.

"Not bad at all, considering I was a little under the weather. Drank too much last night, but Red and I cleared some land," Billy replied. Then, without hesitation, he added, "Hey, Lee drove down some of the roads your boys cut out; pretty fucking sloppy." Lee grinned and did not reply as Robert chuckled at his boy's comment.

"You planning on coming out next week, Pops?" Billy asked as he nodded in acceptance of a beer.

"We'll see. Trying to figure out some contract stuff with the mill and all their corporate horseshit," Robert responded, eyeing the pool table. Then with some slight frustration, he turned to Billy and said, "Now, why don't you go and rack them balls and let's shoot a game."

Billy gave his dad a nod, and then greeted his way around the bar. Ray began pouring the crew their beers. It was the usual late afternoon crowd, same faces, same stories, and same lies. Friday and Saturday nights usually drew some strangers or rare visits from townsfolk. Sometimes mill workers would drive in from Cadillac, a mill town with no bars. Most of the folks who lived there just drank where they wanted to, but sometimes a few guys would come into Hemlock, usually to fight.

The bar was one where generation after generation came to enjoy themselves. Grandsons drank on the same bar stools as their elders did. An old fireplace still provided heat for most of the cold, wet months. It was not uncommon to have the same conversation throughout the bar. Everyone knew everyone else, and if you did not know someone, chances are you quickly became acquaintances.

Billy ordered several shots of whiskey and began to pass them to his crew.

"Drink 'em up, men, and don't get used to the service," Billy shouted as he threw back his shot. It was not uncommon for Billy and Robert to buy drinks for the crew. Robert was the boss, and when he was not around, everyone looked up to Billy. Ray owned the place, but the McDonoughs kept it in business. Drinks were a worker's bonus. No one ever seemed to complain about it either.

"Rack them balls!" Robert yelled in a half drunken roar. He was already near deaf from running saw and equipment for 30 years.

"We called first game," one of the choker boys responded.

"Bullshit, boys. Just because you got me today, don't mean a damn thing," Billy responded, smiling at his dad.

"That's bullshit, Billy," one said, attempting to hold his ground.

Robert responded even though he did not hear half the conversation. "You boys wanna paycheck? I got 10 guys stronger and faster looking for work."

Billy grabbed both pool sticks with a smirk and handed one to his dad. Robert grabbed the stick, leaned over and broke the balls, sending them in various directions; they sounded like crackling sparks from a cedar fire. The two traded shots for a while. Billy studied his father while the old man shot. His balance was off and his face was aging faster than before. When Robert was not working, he was drinking, and Billy could tell this was hard on him.

Springtime was usually when the crew made a better push. As long as the weather cooperated with them, they could continue producing a fair amount of loads each day, without weather or fire shutdowns. Often for a few weeks in the summer, fire shut down would limit their productivity. Smaller logging outfits were finding it hard to survive. Large, corporate logging companies were beginning to outsource much of their logging operations to cheaper countries. President Reagan's politics certainly did not help the small businessman either. That, and rumors of the mill shutting down in Cadillac, the passing of Boone and Mother, all caused Robert to stress.

Billy turned to the game and realized his dad was making a good run, just a few balls standing on the table. His old man could still focus when he needed to.

"Don't miss, McDonough," yelled Tommy, a rather short, fat, stinky man no one liked, but for some demented reason, he was always in the bar when the boys got off shift.

Robert smiled and paused, then glanced at Billy before responding to Tommy, "Fuck you, Tommy. Go fuck your mother, you white trash sonofabitch."

"I ain't white trash," Tommy responded with a hesitant tone.

Always quick on the draw, Billy yelled back, "Tommy, you got four cars that don't run and a house that moves. You're fucking trash!"

Billy's remark caused an uproar of laughter. Robert laughed so hard that he began coughing violently. One of the choker boys nearly fell off his bar stool in laughter. Red and Lee chuckled as they sipped their drinks. Tommy sat speechless in his corner seat at the bar, unable to come up with a response. Tommy, stupid as he was, was still smart enough not to dig a hole he could not get out of. Instead, Tommy glanced across the bar at Red and told him to shut up.

This was not a good idea, but lucky for Tommy, Red was in a good mood and the drinks had not yet absorbed into his Black-foot Indian blood. Red was one of the better fallers around, and had spent most of his life in the area after moving there as a young man from the plains. Nevertheless, once he had a few drinks in him, he was rather unpredictable. Robert and Red more than once found themselves wrestling on the barroom floor. Indeed, everyone at one point in time had to defend himself from Red.

Shaking his head at Tommy, he smiled and gladly ordered another drink, as if to fuel something that did not need any gas. Lee jumped in and began asking Red random questions to interrupt the stare down. For some reason, Tommy was still agitated, though he remained silent.

3

Robert missed an easy shot and shook his head, knowing that his son needed only one more chance to take him. He was right, too. Billy set his drink down and began his run of clearing the table. Billy smiled at his father, who smiled back and gave the nod to the choker boys for a match. The younger of the two got up and walked confidently toward the table. Robert walked toward Red and Lee after glancing at Tommy momentarily. Tommy appeared to be getting a little drunk.

Robert was feeling better than he had earlier, but Tommy had a way of pissing him off. He found himself staring at Tommy, waiting for a mistake to be made. Lee and Red were talking sports, pussy and logging as Robert drifted away, nodding only when the two asked an opinion.

His drink was finished and Robert ordered another. Robert McDonough was legendary throughout the county as a stubborn man who ran a good crew. He had done it for years and even when crews were short, the industry showing its declines, he always made sure he got the job done. Family and work were two areas where no one ever questioned his sincerity. But of late, both worlds were crashing down around him. Work took too much effort and his family was nearly all gone. His brothers never made it to 50, all dying younger in wars, work and bottles. He was raised in a different generation than many of the folks around the woods today. All the men making decisions now never spent a day out in the woods. Big companies had taken over and the big trees were beginning to disappear.

Growing up, he logged with outdated equipment seven days a week for many years. All there ever needed to be was work and family. Times were changing. Rumors of mill closings around the state and in Cadillac were a regular debate in the bars, woods and stores, wherever you went. A concern was in the air.

Ray placed Robert's drink on the table and gave him the typical nod. Robert reached for the drink and noticed his hand shaking more than normal. Years of drinking made him tremble a little, and running saw for more than 30 years gave him white finger, a type of numbness common among folks who run saw for a long while. He rubbed his trigger hand, hoping no one had seen him grimace. He glanced at the pool table and watched as the choker boy complained about his back hurting him. Robert shook his head and could not take it anymore.

"Your fucking back hurts now?" he yelled at the kid. "First it's the pool game and now it's the back." He slid off his bar stool and stood up. "Men never complained about a damn backache. Hell, Red even cut with a busted hand…I tell you what, let me tell you a story about pain." Everyone nearby stopped and listened. The old man was a good storyteller, and most of them were pretty damn honest.

"When Billy was just a kid, I think he was around six, him and his two brothers were playing outside when I came off shift early. Their mother knew something was wrong, because I was there early. She came out to the truck in a hurry, bless her heart, because I cut my damn shoulder nearly off. Fucking saw kicked back and sliced my shoulder damn near into the bone."

He paused momentarily and smiled. "I remember the look on my boys' faces. They stopped playing and stood frozen. I didn't realize it at the time 'cause I was angry, but my shirt was full of blood; it was all over the place. But, I stormed into the house, went in the room and cleaned the sonofabitch right there on my bed. Grabbed some sewing stuff and tried to sew it myself, but Billy's mother had to help me out. Boy, I was angry. We needed the money, so I got back up in the morning and went back to work that next day. Had to sneak some whiskey 'cause it hurt so damn bad, but that day was the first day I ran a loader."

Robert changed his expression, thought for a second and frowned. "Now, think about that next time you complain about your back, kid."

Everyone who was listening to the story stared in various directions for a few seconds, then began talking and doing what they had been doing before Robert had told his story. Billy smiled at the choker boy across the pool table. "True fucking story; I remember the day," he said. The boy leaned over to shoot, keeping his mouth shut. It was the last time anyone heard about his back.

4

Friday nights at the bar were always entertaining. Twice a month, bands would come to play from the larger cities in the valley. Sometimes people would travel with the band down to Ray's place, depending on how good the band was. Those nights, more women would stop in and no one on the crew ever missed the nights bands played. Dancing and laughter would always ensue, ending in a fun night for many, or at least the ones not at the losing end of a fight.

Billy always enjoyed bullshitting with old high school friends, ex-girlfriends, mill workers, or hopeful one-night standers. He was momentarily alone when he recognized an old friend walking in who saw Billy right away. The two men collided in a hug and laughs. Billy knew John from high school. John left town to teach just a few hours away, and rarely had any contact with the town anymore.

"Hey, where is your brother? I don't see him here," John said as he smiled and ordered his first beer. Billy stared at the floor, feeling his father turn his attention to the conversation.

"You still smoke, John?" Billy responded with a blank stare.

"Yeah, sure, you want one?"

"Yeah, let's have one out on the back deck," Billy replied, looking his father in the face that again showed his sadness.

They walked outside and suddenly were alone. The band was just setting up inside and the crowd was still rather small. The back deck had seen better days, but made for a good escape for smoking joints or quiet conversations.

"Did I say something wrong, Billy?" John asked as he handed Billy a Winston.

"No, it's just that Boone died a few months ago," Billy said as he lit his smoke, exhaled and stared into the flame.

John shook his head. "Fuck, man, I'm sorry. I had no idea."

"That's all right, John. Thanks for the smoke."

"What happened?" John asked.

Normally Billy would have ignored the conversation and changed it to something meaningless, where he would not have to enter the emotions and anger that usually followed. But, instead he took another drag and let the smoke rise above him.

"He died in the woods. Pops was running the loader that day and Boone walked underneath it. Pops never knew he was there; ran right over him."

He paused for a moment, then continued, "We were up there nearly two hours before an ambulance arrived, but it was two hours too late. Boone died in Dad's arms, broken in a hundred pieces, bloody. Fuck! There was a lot of blood."

"Jesus Christ, Billy," John said, wide eyed with concern.

"I was cutting on a different landing at the time. I guess Boone was bucking and limbing logs and Pops just did not see him. He couldn't see out the damn window and Boone was swept under the tread."

Billy paused, never making eye contact with John. "And then, go fucking figure, my mother dies three weeks later from cancer. All this shit happening at once, no time to think; everything is just fucked up now."

The two men stood silently, staring at their feet, listening to the laughter from inside the bar and the sounds of gravel being pinched by cars arriving in the parking lot. John looked up at Billy and studied his old friend. He looked bigger and more rugged than he recalled. His arms were large and well defined; his pants still dirty from a day of work.

Billy cleared his throat and spoke, "It's fucked up, John. I remember dropping this tree at the time of the accident and I slipped when it was taking off, and I remember looking over at it when it landed. The fucker shot right back at the stump and nicked my damn helmet. Not but two minutes later, Red is yelling at me from across the ridge. So I get up, thinking I just shit my pants, you know, make sure I wasn't bleeding. I mean, this was really fucking close. I get up and walk toward Red. He was winded. I couldn't understand a damn thing he was saying, but I could not hear any equipment running either. So we ran down towards the crew and there was everyone standing silent. Pops was on the ground rocking Boone back and forth. It was ugly, man. He was choking on his blood, his eyes were lost, staring off to nothing. First time I ever saw my dad cry."

John flicked his smoke into the blackberries off the deck and threw his arms around Billy. Billy began to tense up, trying not to cry. "So sorry for you, Billy. I feel like an asshole. I had no idea. Damn, I'm so sorry."

"It's all right, John. Better take your arms down before someone thinks we're a bunch of queers."

They both laughed at each other and separated. Billy took one last drag of a smoke as he learned across the rail to see what cars were arriving. A few younger women were walking toward the bar from the parking lot. The sight of women helped distract Billy's mind.

"Fuck, looks like we got some talent showing up tonight. Put your game face on, John," Billy said with a smile. "Let's grab another beer, eh?"

"Sounds good, Billy," John replied in a somber voice.

They entered the bar, where another high school friend greeted Billy. John walked over to Robert to shake his hand and pay his respects. Billy watched the front door as the two ladies walked in. The two women felt the looks as if every living being in the bar had glanced in their direction and stared. They walked slowly toward Ray and ordered drinks as the band's drummer greeted them. Everyone resumed their conversations and pool games once the ladies sat down.

"You and me taking shots right now!" his old football friend yelled at Billy, even though they were standing next to each other.

"Hell, Mike, if you'd be buying, I'll be trying," Billy responded.

"You know I saw Annie today at the store," his friend said as he smelled his shot before tossing it back.

"What?" Billy asked, turning around to look at his buddy.

"Yep, there she was. She was talking with her mom. Fuck, she looked good, too."

"You talk to her?" Billy asked, giving Mike his full attention. He had only seen her just a few times since she left town, and left his arms, a mere ten years ago.

"She smiled at me, but I just walked on by. She seemed uninterested."

"Holy shit," Billy whispered with a smile. His heart began to race in anticipation. What a weird day, he thought to himself as he took his friend's shot and tossed it back.

The whiskey went down slow and rough, and Billy began to feel the long, tiring effects of a day's work and a night's drunk. The boom box cried an upbeat country tune as the band went on break. The front door kept swinging open, and more and more people kept pouring in. Billy was beginning to get sick of talking to the same people and decided to challenge an old man to a game of pool. He was a retired postmaster who often found himself at that bar almost as much as he did when he worked a shift. As he was racking the pool balls, he noticed two women walk in. One was Annie, the other her old high school friend and Hemlock grade school teacher, Susie.

With a smile, Annie first greeted Robert, who was sitting near the door still arguing with Red and Lee about something meaningless. Billy was on the other side of the bar, but it did not take long before their eyes met. Annie smiled at Billy and began walking toward him.

Billy set down his pool stick and tried to move in her direction. They began to cut between conversations and battled around standing drunks to greet one another. Billy watched as Annie walked closer, his eyes drifting up and down her body. She could tell he had been in the bar awhile, as he often caught his balance with the help of others in the way. He stared with an interested smirk that turned to a large smile.

But before they could meet, a fight broke out between the choker boys and some Cadillac mill workers. Beer glasses were thrown and pool sticks were snapped on heads. Annie got shoved aside by one of the mill workers as he tried to engage in the fight.

Billy rushed toward Annie, but was intercepted with a shove. Annie turned to Susie and quickly fled out the door, as the fight grew louder. It was broken up rather quickly as Billy ran toward the front door helping toss the mill workers out of the bar. Once outside, Billy saw Annie walking toward Susie's truck.

"Go home and get out of here," Billy shouted to the drunken, wounded mill workers.

"Fuck you, motherfucker," one replied as he held his nose in place, blood running in between his cupped fingers.

"Yeah, yeah, all right, get the fuck outta here," Billy said as he looked at Annie, who impatiently looked back at him.

"How are you?" Billy asked Annie in a half drunken, breathless voice.

"I can see nothing has changed here," she responded in a rather sober and impatient manner.

"Well, come back in and I'll buy you a drink. C'mon, it will be fun. We can catch up on things. . I mean, how are you, what are you doing here?" Billy foolishly said, slightly nervous.

Realizing this, Annie grinned, no longer angry, but still somewhat impatient. "Well, I quit my job and I have not been home since my dad died, so I figured I would take a couple weeks and see if Mom needed any help," she said.

"So, you will be around for awhile. Wow, that's great," Billy said, lacking a creative thought, unable to stare at her long enough to study her natural beauty.

Susie was sitting in the driver's seat, smoking a cigarette and watching as the two talked. She watched as Annie studied Billy, looking at his dress and figure. Billy lifted his head momentarily in the silence to look at Annie, causing him to smile, as if to telepathically tell Annie his thoughts.

Annie was thin and tall, and she took good care of herself. Her dark hair rested at a good length and she wore it in a way that exposed her face. Her skin appeared slightly bronze, but Billy could not really tell in the evening streetlights. He recalled her subtle beauty and her presence, something she still carried with her. Annie's eyes left Billy long enough to stare off into the evening sky.

Billy interrupted her daze. "Well, I'm amazed, but you look more gorgeous than ever."

"Thank you, Billy. You look bigger than I remember you last. I guess it's been a few years."

Billy tried to fill the silence with something halfway interesting to say, but he could not find it. He took his eyes off her once again to stare at the ground, and began drawing designs with his feet in the gravel. In the distance, tires skidded around a turn, causing him to lift his head and glance at her with a smile.

Robert noticed Billy's struggles as he viewed this conversation from indoors. He quickly ordered a few beers and stumbled outside, handing one to Annie, the other to Billy. Annie replied with a smile, though it appeared she had been ready to go. Robert smiled back and asked Susie to join him in the bar for a drink. Robert reached gently for Susie's hand and smiled, giving an obvious wink to Billy. The two walked to the bar, leaving Billy and Annie alone.

"Your dad looks tired. How is he?" Annie asked after taking a sip. She waited for Billy's response, watching as he swallowed a third of the beer in one sip.

"Well, it's been a tough year. Boone and Mom died this winter, so other than that, I guess he is all right," Billy replied, gazing at his feet.

"I'm sorry, Billy. My mom told me a while back. I should have sent my wishes. How are you holding up?" Annie's voice became softer and much sweeter. She reached over and lightly placed her hand on Billy's arm, trying to be as sincere as possible. She could feel the strength of his muscles. Long, laborious hours of harsh work helped shape him into what stood before her. His arms surprised her, and she stood back and looked, gazing at his unshaven face. She felt a brief chill, then a rush of blood, and her heart beginning to beat a little faster.

Billy interrupted her moment of attraction and said, "I guess I'm all right. Trying to stay busy with work." The comment caught Annie off guard and she took a second to recall her original question. She could tell that Billy did not want to talk about the loss and she did not press it. The two learned against the truck and silently gazed at the stars.

Annie began talking about how nice it was to breathe some fresh air and to be outside in the quiet night. Billy's mind began to wander. He thought about throwing Annie in the cab and taking her right then and there—just like the old days, when they were saturated in careless love and curious sex. He began to backtrack, and could recall her smells and moans, their bodies touching each other naked, sweating, and the soothing sounds of her sleep. It had been 10 years since they split the sheets, but even with a heavy head, he could clearly recall those moments.

"Have you been listening to me?" Annie said, interrupting Billy's thoughts and glaring at his eyes.

He grinned, returned the stare, and said cautiously, "Of course. Of course I have been."

"Well, are there any women in your life?"

"No one in particular," Billy grinned. "Hell, I heard you were engaged."

"I was until I realized he was an asshole."

"Probably so," Billy said in agreement.

"Why do you say that?" Annie asked in a frowning manner.

"I don't know," was his only response.

Susie appeared, walking toward the two of them as they continued to lean against her truck. She had darted out of the bar rather fast and both could tell she was agitated. Obviously, too many men inside probably tried one thing or another to get her going the way she was. She broke pace near Annie and asked if she needed a lift home. Annie agreed and handed Billy the half empty beer with a smile.

"Whatdayamean you're going home?" Billy said in a confused voice.

"I'll be around," Annie said.

She opened the truck door and gave Billy one last friendly glance before giving Susie her attention. Billy grabbed both beers and started walking toward the bar.

"Well, I'll be damned," he mumbled as he walked closer to the bar. Again speaking barely loud enough for himself to hear, he said, "What a weird fucking night."

"You pussy. Should've been fucking that tonight," one of the choker boys yelled as he pissed on a tire in the parking lot.

"Guess there is always tomorrow," Billy replied in a rather somber voice.

5

"What happened inside the bar, Sue?" Annie asked as she reached for the seat belt.

"One of those perverts grabbed my ass. They know I am married, fucking assholes!" Susie barked, still agitated as her truck headed east down Main Street toward their old high school.

"How's Billy doing? He seemed a little drunk," Susie said as she made a left turn up a hill toward Annie's mother's house.

"Yeah, I think he was pretty wasted," Annie replied, pausing and thinking about their conversation. "He seems okay, I guess, all things considered."

"Yeah, he's had it pretty rough lately," Susie said as she turned and began slowing down in front of the house.

Annie briefly studied her mother's yard, which appeared neglected. The house needed new paint, the deck was beginning to rot after another wet winter, and the fence was missing some posts.

"Do you ever get depressed here?" Annie asked, turning her attention back to Susie.

"Well, yes, but I have found myself going to the valley more often and doing some things. School is keeping me real busy. I know what you are saying. Sometimes I come back here after going camping during the summer or doing something outside of town for awhile, and I want to cry," Susie replied, briefly clenching the steering wheel, feeling embarrassed for never leaving.

She turned her attention back to Annie. "Why did you leave Seattle?" she asked.

Annie looked down and saw a faint tan line on her left ring finger. She lifted her head with a smile. "I don't know. I wasn't happy there. The guy I was with gave me everything, but I felt hollow. Absent in a way, you know?"

Susie was shaking her head, as if to say she understood. Annie continued, "Not sure why, I guess, but I needed time away. I just walked out and left. I'm thinking about maybe going down to California somewhere. I just want to take it easy, but I don't know where to do that. Mom is depressing and this town is depressing. I don't know."

"Well, if you stay long, you will get sucked into the hole here. Trust me, it looks hard, but it's easy. The best thing you did was go away far away to college," Susie said in her serious teacher tone.

"I know. I don't think I will have any trouble leaving here soon," Annie replied, looking at the dilapidated home where had she had grown up.

6

The morning came early for Billy. He lifted his heavy head from his pillow, slowly rolled over, and drank the remaining water that he had brought to bed with him. He sat up, half naked, rubbed his eyes, and began to ponder how he had made it home. He opened the window shade and peered outside. The sun was beginning to shine through the tall fir trees, and it appeared the rain had stopped just in time to welcome the morning.

As he left his bedroom, he took the time to notice the house was a mess. No one was around to clean up after the two of them. Billy had moved back into the house once his mother found out she had cancer. But since her passing, he began working more and more, and spending more time away at the bar. Robert was rarely around, and was not educated on household chores. He had relied on his wife all his life to tend to the house.

Stacks of beer cans and empty whiskey bottles lined the table and countertops. The trash was overflowing and ready to be burned, but no one had managed the meager effort to take it outside. Billy scratched his chest and shook his head, as he could smell his dad, who appeared to have been putting in some quality time in the bathroom.

Billy threw on a sweater, grabbed the trash and took it to the burn pile. He could not take it any longer; someone had to step it up. While outside he stopped momentarily, pulled his underwear down and began taking his morning piss, staring out into the underbrush and tall fir trees. Everything was very fresh and clean, as if God had just given the earth a car wash.

Billy turned around and studied the house. Robert and his brothers had built the home several years ago. Its outside was covered with cedar shingles and had decks surrounding the single story. It had high ceilings that gave it a roomy atmosphere. Large windows captured the limited light the tall trees allowed in. A small creek paralleled the house just a few meters away and ran year round, and at times provided good swimming holes further upstream. Billy walked in and began searching for some coffee.

Inside the home, when it was clean, gave a feeling of comfort. A large wood stove provided heat most of the year. The walls and floor were covered in wood. Photos of family and logging moments lined the walls, giving a visual history of the trade and the family. But for all its comforts, the house had been neglected recently.

Billy had dated a very kind Mexican gal named Maria just a few months ago, but she turned out to be an illegal immigrant and was sent on a bus heading south. Some asshole from town got wind of it and the sheriff had nothing better to do but get involved. Billy had begun to like having her around. She worked part time at the local café waiting tables, which allowed a lot of time for her to hang around the house and cook and clean.

At first, Robert did not like having a Mexican in the house, but after a few home-cooked meals and her cleaning efforts, his close-minded remarks quickly turned into welcoming ones. She was a sweet woman who spoke only enough English to get by. Oftentimes Billy would come home to her listening to some Mexican music. He found it funny, cute in a way. She would be singing at the top of her lungs and dancing around the house, almost as a form of escape; an escape that made her think of her own country, the dirt streets and dust, the heat, garbage burning in the distance, the sounds of roosters singing in the morning, stray dogs on the prowl, and homemade tortillas. Billy would often walk in quietly and watch her before announcing his presence with a slap on her ass or a quick attack on the fridge. She was content to be helping out and making a few dollars at the café. There were not too many Mexicans around Hemlock, so she felt a little out of place. At times, she would feel the eyes of store clerks watching her, assuming she'd steal if given the opportunity. But for the most part, she ignored the stereotypes and went about her business.

One time Billy ran into one of his past co-workers, who gave him some shit for sleeping with a Mexican. Billy did his best to ignore it. He and Maria were at the hardware store buying some things when his old friend ran his mouth. Maria walked away, saddened by the man's remarks, and waited in the truck. Billy gave his friend one last warning to shut his mouth, but the guy would hear nothing of it. For some damn reason, it was more important to run his mouth and make his point, so Billy ended the conversation with one punch, sending his old friend backwards into the paint cans. He collided with the cans hard enough to knock several over and make a mess. The store clerks just shook their heads at Billy and showed their disgust. Billy was embarrassed with the argument and apologized to his friends who ran the store. He had nothing against a woman who wore brown skin; it did not matter at all to him.

He met her at the café in town. She was living with her brother at the time, but it was not long before she moved into their house. Having her around made the absence of Boone and his mother much easier to deal with. She was attracted to Billy, but it was almost her responsibility to help out with him and his dad. When the news of Boone hit town, followed by the death of his mother, Maria wanted to help. She did so by cooking them dinners and keeping them company. Many of the authentic Mexican dishes were hard to make, as no one carried any decent ingredients, but Maria was still able to impress the men with some quality meals and a nourishing presence.

She had left a few of her records behind. Billy made a cup of coffee, leaned over and put on one of her records. He could not make out the writing, but it was one she used to sing and dance to around the house. He set the needle on the vinyl and the crackling Mexican band starting playing. The music was a bit annoying to him that morning, but it made him think back.

Robert even took notice as he shouted from the bathroom, "Maria, is that you?"

"No, Pops, just playing her record," Billy said as he tried to read the writing on the back of the record cover.

"Shit," was Robert's only response.

The house that Billy grew up in began to get more and more uncomfortable. For some reason, it started to bother Billy. He could feel the emptiness now more than ever, and drafts would catch him cold and off guard. The winds and rain seemed to make different sounds at night, throwing shadows in the air, making him second-guess his steps and sanity. His father did not help either. He played as if he had everything together, even when he took time off to drink at the bar, but the truth was evident to Billy. His dad was careless with his evidence. The old Colt was sitting on the coffee table; the picture of Boone still sat on the sofa. Normally the gun remained in the bedroom and the pictures on the wall. Billy tried to ignore it and pretended not to notice. His dad finished up and the smell drifted its unpleasant scent throughout the house.

"Damn whiskey shits, fucking nasty," Robert said as he carried the morning paper out with him.

"Yeah, I can feel it beginning to brew," Billy said in response, nodding toward the gun.

Robert picked up on his evidence and ignored it momentarily before saying, "There it is. I was gonna clean the thing yesterday, but I never got around to it."

Billy could tell his dad was lying. His face showed him everything he needed as proof. His father could tell tall tales to many, but his own son picked up on his lies rather quickly. Billy was too tired and sore to say anything further. Though concerned, he turned toward the kitchen and grabbed the cast iron pan. "Hey, you want any eggs?"

"Sure, sounds good. You drink all the coffee?" Robert asked as he picked up the gun and examined it.

"Nah, there's a little left; one more cup maybe."

7

Mother was good around the house. She would do all the cooking and cleaning, and enjoyed looking after her three boys and husband. Raising three kids and putting up with Robert's stubbornness was a full-time job. All three boys were alike, but also had their own different interests. She always tried to please them and encouraged their interests, whereas Robert's parenting was rather blunt and simple.

She'd met Robert in high school and quickly fell in love. Little had changed over the 30 years they were married. Both had grown up in Hemlock and enjoyed the quietness of the town. The McDonough family was successful within the Hemlock community and always had been. Once a larger family, the McDonoughs had always run its own logging outfit. She knew things were changing and could see that many in the community ignored what was obvious. She secretly hated the fact that her boys worked in the woods. Logging was one of the few good jobs around, but deep down she did not like the danger. All her boys were intelligent and she felt they could have embarked on other things.

In Robert's mind, there was working in the woods - and all the other stuff for other people. The love-hate relationship with the woods was always there, but being with her family was the most important. Watching as her boys and husband devour a meal she made would bring her comfort, and knowing that they would do anything she asked around the house at any time helped her believe she had done a good job raising her kids.

Wood was always present in the McDonough boys' lives. Robert had the kids chopping wood at a very young age, and as they grew into teenagers, all were handy with chainsaws. Robert Junior had resisted logging. He had always helped out, but only seemed to do the bare minimum. He listened to his dad explain how to sharpen the teeth of the chain and clean the saw, but it did not stick the way it did for Billy and Boone. If they went out to cut firewood, Junior was usually the first to quit stacking wood or cutting trees. Robert was never very impressed with his older boy, and it was not uncommon to hear the two of them arguing throughout much of Junior's adolescence.

Junior was just a year older than Billy, but his imagination was light years ahead. He did not like the living that was expected of him from his father. He was a good student in high school, and would often hide in his room reading newspapers and books that he would check out at the school library. Photographs of large cities and endless possibilities helped blur his frustration with his father and small-town mentalities. Mother secretly encouraged Junior to read and look beyond Hemlock. She wanted Junior to go to college and continue to learn. Anything, she thought, would be better than following Robert's footsteps.

After graduation, he left for college in New York City, where he fell in love with the sights and sounds of the fast-paced metropolis. He would write his mother once a month and give her updates from the city. He would describe his experiences with college and meeting nice girls, tall buildings and museums, different colors of people and foods. Mother would have his letters set aside at the post office so Robert would not know of her communication with her oldest boy. Robert never would talk about his firstborn within the family or at the bar. In his mind, he was long gone, over a decade since he had seen his kid. He knew that everyone had contact with him, but he was too stubborn to ask about his boy. He had left and that was all there was. Junior had returned several times, but only to see his brothers and mother.

There would be times when folks would come over for a barbecue or some gathering and inquire about the extra kid in some of the family photos. Robert would always walk away and let Mary or one of his boys answer the question. Everyone thought Robert's behavior was rather ridiculous, but stubbornness ran in the family, and Junior certainly never made an effort to reconcile.

8

Annie woke up that morning to hear her mother coughing and the sounds of a lighter scratching—her failed attempts to light her morning smoke. The scratches stopped, her cough did not, and soon the smell of cigarette smoke drifted into her bedroom. Annie peered at the wristwatch that lay next to her on the lamp table.

"Wow, it's late," she whispered, smacking her mouth in disgust at her dry throat.

She sat erect and closed her eyes tightly. Annie stretched forward, placing her hands on the bridges of her feet. There was nothing that required immediate attention, but Annie felt the need to get up and do something. For years now, her high-paced lifestyle had made Annie feel as if she always needed to do something. She put a pair of sweat pants over her exposed legs, then grabbed a pair of clean socks out of her suitcase and slipped into them. Opening the door to the living room exposed her to a hazy cloud of smoke.

"Good morning, Ma," she said as she ran her hands through her hair.

"There's coffee in the kitchen if you want some. I don't know if you still drink it," her mom said as she read the morning *Oregonian.*

"Yes, even people in Seattle drink coffee, Mom," Annie replied in a sarcastic tone, causing her mother to again lower the paper and give her daughter a look.

Annie yawned as she walked toward the kitchen. She served herself a cup of coffee, sat down at the kitchen table and looked outside. The sun was shining in between a few high clouds. The steam remained on the windows from the coffee pot and recent rains. The lawn was wet from the evening's brief shower, making it look more depressing, as no one had attended to it in a while. Shaking her head, she walked toward the refrigerator, opened it up, and glanced inside. It was empty and had a smell of stale milk. She grabbed the milk and took a sniff. It was sour; the expiration date read weeks ago. Suddenly the coffee she drank did not sit very well in her stomach.

"Hey, Mom, is the store open yet?"

"Yes, it opens at six," her mother responded, then returned with, "why, are you hungry? There are some donuts near the bread box."

Annie glanced over in that direction. She grabbed a sugar-coated donut with renewed energy and ate away.

"Where is the lawn mower?" Annie asked, still in the kitchen, her mouth half full of donut.

"It broke down awhile back." Pausing, her mother wrestled with the newspaper. "Why, do you want to mow the lawn?"

"It just looks like shit, that's all," Annie replied, staring outside once again. "Can I borrow your truck, Mom?"

"What for?"

"I want to go to the store," Annie replied, feeling that she needed to contribute to the house. Buying some groceries was the first step. She was actually surprised that her mom, who worked at the store, had no groceries.

"Yeah, I guess. I have to work at noon. I'm covering for Bev today."

"No problem, Mom. I will be back soon," Annie said as she entered the living room and looked over at her mother. She headed to the bathroom and washed her face, then began brushing her teeth as she sat on the toilet. She played with her hair as she stared into the mirror, taking a deep breath, sighing in irritation.

"What am I doing here?" she asked herself in the mirror.

Waiting momentarily, as if she would receive a response, she opened the door and walked into her room. She pulled her sweats and underwear off, and slipped into some new clothes. Her jeans slipped on tight and hugged her thin, long legs. She threw on her sweatshirt and walked back into the living room.

"Where are the keys at, Mom?"

"Over on the table where my purse is."

"Okay, see you later. Hey, what do you want for dinner?"

"Whatever you want to cook is alright with me."

"Okay, Mom. Bye," Annie said, casting a smile toward the older woman, who lowered the paper to watch her daughter leave. Before Annie could close the front door, she raised her voice, "You know, Billy may have a lawn mower."

Annie paused for a second and tilted her head, searching for a response. She did not have one and exited the house, walking carefully to avoid the jungle-like grass. She wrestled with the keys and tapped the gas pedal. The truck coughed a few times before firing up. Annie bounced around the cab briefly trying to warm herself while the truck did the same. Moments later, she headed down the hill toward the store.

She drove by homes and studied them briefly as her truck wobbled along. The brakes screeched at every stop sign, as Annie spent more time looking at the homes and yards than the back streets of Hemlock. Many of the homes were beginning to show signs of wear and tear. Once or twice a block, a well kept home would separate itself from the worn-down look of Hemlock.

The store appeared along Main Street, but for some reason Annie did not feel like stopping. She had a more enjoyable time sightseeing, recalling past days of running through the streets, and the various homes she use to visit for trick-or-treating or high school parties. She headed through town and found herself escaping the shops and stores and again returning to the residential areas. Crossing a bridge, she took another road that headed out of town. She smiled in recognition. It was the way to Billy's house, a road she had been down a thousand times before. Following the creek by the roadside, she began to carve her way through the tall trees.

9

Billy began cleaning up some of the beer cans that had started to take over the counter. He cursed as he attempted to bring a little life back into the house. He had ground some more coffee and impatiently waited as the blackened filtered water slowly dripped into the aged, stained coffee pot. The dog sat and watched his owner struggle with domestic affairs, waiting for Billy to realize his presence and let him outside. Billy noticed Hank's impatience when the dog finally gave in and started moaning in frustration. Billy looked down at the dog's food bowl and noticed it was empty. He reached for the bag of dog food and poured his friend a healthy dose of grub. Watching his dog, he got distracted from cleaning and instead poured himself a cup of coffee. Hank had eaten a few mouthfuls of food, but he was not interested any longer. He strutted toward the door and looked back at Billy. Smiling, Billy walked over and the two wandered outside where they could both relieve themselves. Hank jumped off the deck and found a tree. Billy walked toward the edge of the deck and the two peed together.

The morning sunshine did bring some warmth, but the weather was still cool. Billy slurped his coffee and walked over to the woodpile, picked up the splitting maul and began cutting firewood. His mind began to drift as sweat started to bead up on his forehead, releasing some of the toxins from the night before. Occasionally, he would smell a faint whiff of whiskey in between chops, shaking his head as he went. Billy had always believed that work and sweat were the best medications for a hangover, and today his theories were true.

He was creating a rhythm with each chop, and focused on nothing but his cutting. He'd set one log up, cut it, grab another, and do the same again. When the cut pieces began piling up too high, he threw them aside and did it all over again. Billy would pause only long enough to wipe his brow and briefly straighten his back. Hank patiently watched as his master cut through pieces of wood, bringing Billy a stick from time to time so he could help in the cause. Billy would throw the stick as far as he could to get a few moments alone. Hank would sometimes go for a smaller log and try and move it around, having little luck. Either way, the project kept the two occupied for the time being.

Robert wandered out to the living room after he heard noises out near the woodshed. He peered out the kitchen window to see his boy cutting wood. Shaking his head in approval, he poured himself another cup of dark black coffee. Hank, now bored from running, walked up on the deck and waited for Robert to open the door, eagerly shaking his tail for the food that awaited him. Robert walked over to the door and opened it softly, as if not wanting to interrupt Billy. He then walked toward his living room chair and sat down, content. He looked over at his dog with a smile.

"You know, Hank, I just had me a wonderful shit, how 'bout you?" Hank did nothing in response but eat his remaining food. Robert chuckled again and continued to read the paper.

A truck pulled into the driveway and slowly came to a stop as its tires pinched the gravel below it. Annie quietly got out and saw Billy near the woodshed. Billy had his back to her and apparently had not seen her arrive. He continued to cut and toss wood as Annie walked toward him. Billy wiped his sweat once again before taking his shirt off to use as a towel, coughing briefly in response to the smell of his shirt. He then tossed it aside on the cut firewood.

Annie came to a halt just a few yards away and waited a few minutes to watch Billy slice through the large logs as if it took no effort. She began to lose herself in thought, watching her old love tear through wood, sending the shattered pieces in opposite directions. She had gotten used to the well-dressed, well-spoken men of the city, and had forgotten about how things were around here. She had suppressed many of her memories of Hemlock. Billy had entered her mind at various times throughout the last decade, but until now, she had not been at all attracted to this kind of sight. She studied as Billy lifted the heavy splitting maul over his head and with a fast, quick release, smacked it down the center of the logs.

His upper body had grown more muscular than what she recalled. With each swing, his arms and back exposed his muscles from long hours of physical work. This caused a smile from Annie, who still leaned against the tree and enjoyed the view. She was not used to this kind of morning.

10

Annie had been engaged for eight months, and at the time was saturated in love. Her man was a successful corporate lawyer and worked long hours. He would often surprise Annie with random expensive gifts and tropical vacations. Though her life was filled with possessions and a caring man, it was also controlled by routines, work, vacations, even sex.

The two had been together for just over a year, and had made handfuls of friends around Seattle, people they regularly met for cocktails. Annie was caught up in the city scene and never once looked back. The quiet streets of Hemlock were long gone, and rooftop apartments and upscale restaurants replaced her old home. She was happily distracted at the time and it seemed as if she were content.

But since her father died, she had a slightly different outlook. Her brief return to Hemlock for her father's funeral certainly did not attract her to the idea of moving back, but it put some things in perspective for her. She began thinking about a change, simplifying things in a way she had not thought about in a long while.

Her last night in Seattle, Annie waited at home, sipping scotch and staring at the large diamond on her hand. The ring once pleased her, but on that night, it made her ill. She began to pace around the lonely apartment, looking at the photographs of her with her fiancé. The photos displayed the two of them sitting in lawn chairs in Mexico and cafes in France sipping wine. She rested her glass on the fireplace and looked around the room at its leather couches and glass tables, marble benches and crystal dishes put perfectly in their place to enhance their importance. This all meant something to Annie, who graduated college broke. But she was determined to move up in the world. She had gotten accustomed to city life and the money that was required to live comfortably there. Yet for some reason, things were beginning to change.

She began to feel nauseated and went to the bedroom to sit on the bed. She stared into her walk-in closet long enough to see her suitcase. She popped up off the bed and began tossing some clothes into the suitcase. Grabbing a pen and paper, she wrote the most heartfelt letter she could to her fiancé, explaining the reasons for leaving. She really did not know why she was doing this, but told him she was heading back to her mother's house for a while to think about things. For some reason, it took only a glass of scotch and few quiet minutes of thought to convince her to take a break.

For one reason or another, she was struck with an uncomfortable uncertainty about her life that night, so she acted on it, something she had always done. She left the note and the ring on the kitchen table. Closing the door, she looked back at her home with sadness, then struggled to carry her suitcases down the hallway toward the elevator.

11

Still silent, she continued to lean against the tree, watching as Billy cut wood. She was impressed and entertained. In the past, it was a man's political outlook or his educational background that impressed her, but today it was the simple sight of a man sweating and working with his hands.

"How are you feeling?" she said, interrupting Billy, who missed the piece of wood, hitting the maul handle on the wood instead.

Billy stumbled over a few pieces of wood, surprised by someone's voice, let alone Annie's. "How long you been standing there?" he asked as he regained his balance.

"Long enough to watch you sweat," she said with a grin.

"Oh yeah," he replied.

"Do you have a lawn mower?" Annie asked, smiling at Billy as he reached over to grab his shirt. He put it back on, though it was sweaty by now.

"You come out here just to ask if I had a lawn mower?" Billy said as he began to cool down and feel the wet shirt against his back.

"Yeah, Mom's lawn looks like shit and Dad's old lawn mower doesn't work."

"Who's gonna mow the lawn?" Billy asked, as if to question Annie's lawn-mowing capability.

"I am!" Annie replied.

"Won't you break a nail?" Billy asked, smiling.

"Forget it then, never mind," Annie said.

"I got a damn mower. I'll help you bring it over to your mom's house. You know you have not changed a bit, still moody, still spoiled."

"Is that right?" Annie said, folding her arms.

"Yes, it is," Billy replied, staring into Annie's eyes. He was still a little bitter that Annie ran away to college many years ago. He had long been over her, but they had never had a chance to talk or even address the end of their relationship. Her departure had been spontaneous in Billy's mind. Not so in Annie's.

In high school she often talked to Billy about college and moving away. Billy never really paid much attention to the thought. He did not even sign a football scholarship until the last day he could. Long afterward, Annie told him she was moving back east to school. Her departure was sudden. One morning she woke up with Billy after the two had slept in the bed of his truck. They would often go up in the woods by themselves, or sometimes with another couple or two, to camp and mess around. It was a hot August day and she told him that morning when she awoke. Three days later, she left for school in Massachusetts.

"Let me go see if the damn thing has any gas in it," Billy said as he walked into the shed. Annie stood outside. She took the time to examine the property. It looked the same as it did years ago. More moss had grown on the roofs of the house and shed, but it basically looked the same as before.

"You want some coffee?" Robert shouted from the kitchen window toward Annie. Annie smiled in response and waived. "Sure, please!"

Robert fumbled around, trying to find a few clean coffee cups, and poured two cups for his boy and Annie. "What the hell is she doing out here?" he mumbled to himself as he blew the dust off one mug. He struggled to open the door with the two cups in his hand. He walked out to the shed, handed Annie a cup and waited to see what Billy was trying to do.

"What the hell are you doing in there making all that noise?" Robert asked as he smiled at Annie.

"Getting the lawn mower out," Billy said in a frustrated voice.

"Why? We don't gotta lawn anymore," Robert said as he took a sip of his boy's coffee.

"Annie wants to borrow it."

"Oh," Robert said as he smiled again at Annie. "Gonna mow your momma's lawn?"

"Yes. I don't think it has been tended to since my father died."

"How is your momma doing?" Robert asked as he picked up a stick and threw it for Hank. The dog had found his way outside once Robert had opened the door.

"She's the same as always," Annie said.

"Yeah, not much changes around here," Robert said as he watched Hank search for the stick in the nearby brush, then returned his attention to Annie.

"No, it does not seem to change much," Annie said as she looked at Robert. Both of them looked at each long enough to wonder what the other was really trying to say.

"Here it is," Billy said as he pushed it outside.

"Thanks Billy," Annie said, and looked at the mower as if it were some sort of object from outer space.

"No problem. I'll just throw it in your truck and you can bring it back when you are done," Billy said, knowing that she was not comfortable with the exchange. "I put some new gas in it. You should be fine for the lawn you got."

The two walked over to her truck. Annie caressed the coffee mug with two hands as she watched her feet. Billy pushed the mower next to her as he looked her truck over.

"Okay, thanks Billy," Annie said, staring back toward the house. "The house looks good."

"Yeah, well inside is a different story," Billy said as he lifted the lawn mower into her truck. "So, all you wanted was just to borrow the lawn mower?"

"I don't know, I mean, yeah, I want to help around my mom's house, and you were the first person I thought of that could help me out." She paused and looked Billy over. She felt somewhat obligated to do something for him in return. "Do you wanna go out for dinner or grab a drink sometime and talk?"

Shaking his head in approval, he said, "Yeah, that would be good."

Annie walked toward the driver's door and got in. Billy followed her and stopped. "You sure you don't need any help with the lawn? Not doing much around here."

"I'll manage I think," Annie replied as she started the truck, handing Billy her empty coffee cup. "By the way, you stink. You need to shower."

Billy began laughing. "You're still the same, you know that?" He gave her one last friendly glance and walked away laughing. He paused and turned around to watch Annie back the truck up and begin heading back to town.

Robert was still throwing the stick and shouting at the dog. Billy walked in his direction and stared at the woodpile. They both stood silent before Billy said, "Five bucks says she can't start it." Robert laughed and reached for his chew can, took a dip and handed it to Billy. Billy grabbed it and took a pinch.

"I ain't taking that bet," Robert said as he headed back inside. Billy smiled and slammed the splitting maul into a log.

12

Annie soon realized that she should have let Billy help her out. Getting the lawn mower out of the truck was not an easy task. She brought a few bags of groceries into the house instead.

"How is Billy?" her mother asked as she helped put away some of the groceries. Her mom was now fully dressed and ready to run a few errands and go to work.

"How did you know I went to see Billy?" Annie asked, confused, as she put a dozen eggs into the fridge.

"I just figured you would go see him. He's a nice boy, and you have been gone awhile," her mom said, smiling and looking into her daughter's eyes in order to make her point.

"He's good. I borrowed his lawn mower. Can you help me get it out of the truck?"

"I can try," her mother said, coughing as she reached for her cigarettes and matches.

The two walked outside and stared at the lawn mower. "You know how to use this?"

"Sure. It can't be that difficult, just pull the cord and push the damn thing," Annie said, attempting to sound confident.

"Yeah, I think that's it," her mother said as the two each grabbed a side of the lawn mower and dropped it off the tailgate of the truck.

"Okay, I'm off to work. See you later, Annie," her mother said as she walked toward the driver's seat.

"Bye, Mom. I'll see you later," Annie replied as she studied the lawn mower. It was dirty and appeared to have been in the shed for a long while. Old gas and oil spills clouded the instructions for operation. Annie pushed the mower from the driveway to the lawn. She started pulling the starter cord, but was not having much luck, and after a half dozen pulls, she tried to work the choke. She tried again; no luck. She began to get frustrated with the mower and walked away from it, resting her hands on her hips. Focusing again, she walked toward the mower and pulled several more times. It just would not fire. But she was bound to succeed and again studied the machine, wondering what could be wrong with it. Again she pulled the starter cord with no luck. Behind her she could hear a truck coming to a stop. She glanced back and recognized Billy sitting there smiling, watching her struggle.

"How is that working out for ya?" Billy asked.

"What!" Annie yelled back impatiently.

"Looks like you're having some trouble with that," Billy said as he got out of the truck.

"I see you changed your shirt," Annie responded.

"Oh, yeah, well I heard some complaints."

Smiling, Annie watched as Billy walked toward her.

"Here, let me see something," Billy said as he leaned down and looked over the mower. "You need the choke on first."

"I had it that way once before," Annie said as she folded her arms.

"That's all right, it happens a lot," Billy said as he pulled the starter cord. His first attempt did not take, and this brought a smile to Annie's face. However, his second pull fired the mower up, sending a quick burst of dark smoke out the exhaust. Billy let the mower run for a second, looked over at Annie and smiled. "Seems to be running okay now," he remarked with another smile.

"Thanks Billy," Annie said, then frowned as she moved out of the way, knowing that Billy would go ahead and mow the lawn. He was thinking the same thing as he pushed the mower through the thick grass. It stalled out from time to time, but the mower did its job. Within 20 minutes, the lawn was mowed and Billy had gotten another shirt stinky and sweaty. Annie was kind enough to greet Billy with a beer when he finished.

"Thanks for the cold one," Billy said as he took a large gulp.

"Thanks for mowing the lawn, Billy."

"You got a rake? This grass is everywhere," Billy said as he took another sip.

"I think so," Annie responded without much confidence.

They stood together silent for a moment as Billy recovered from his exercise with the aid of the tall can of beer. Annie felt somewhat odd, as she had failed to prove herself to her old friend.

"Don't get down on yourself. This old thing is tough to start," Billy said with a smile.

"I'm not upset, I am just not very strong, I guess," Annie said, laughing as she sipped her beer. "Would you like it if I cooked you and your dad a home-cooked meal sometime? You two seem like you need some company."

"Yeah, that would be nice. It's been a while since we had a lady cooking for us," Billy said.

"Okay, I'll come up with something to make you two and cook it for you guys sometime soon," Annie said as she took another sip and looked across the yard.

Billy finished his beer and threw it in the bed of his truck. He grabbed the mower, lifted it into the bed and shut the tailgate. Then he slapped his hands and wiped them on his pants.

"You ever think about me?" Annie said as she looked at Billy long enough to make eye contact, then settled her eyes on the top of the beer can. Moments of their past had crept into her mind with the taste of beer.

Billy took a deep breath, paused for a moment and looked Annie over, waiting for her to lift her head. He spoke softly. "Why?"

"I was just curious. So much has happened since we were together. I mean we were so young then and now look at us. Ten years has come and gone, and it seems like it was just yesterday." Annie lowered her face again and shook her head. "I don't know."

Billy folded his arms and leaned against his truck, studying the mess of cans and saw equipment in the bed before returning his attention to the question. "You know, a lot of time has come and gone since you went away, Annie." He paused and thought for a second. "I am not the same guy you once knew. I know you drive down these streets and you see the same things, but time has a way of making things disappear."

That was not what Billy wanted to say. He wanted to throw her over his shoulder and bring her inside, get naked and go at it. Just like the old days, like nothing had changed. But he remained reserved and waited for a response.

"What are you thinking right now?" Annie asked as she tilted her head gently to the side and focused on Billy's eyes.

Billy laughed. "You know what I am thinking; that has not changed a bit."

Annie smiled, dropped her arms and returned her eyes toward Billy's. "I better get inside," she said as she took one last sip of beer.

"Okay. I'm sure you have a lot to do today," Billy said as he opened the door to the truck. He could tell now that he stood a good chance of getting Annie in bed. She was back home with nothing really to do. She had just broken up with her fiancé; she was bored and vulnerable. He did not press the issue too much. He knew she'd come around.

"Listen, I told one of my old friends that lives in Salem that I would go visit her tonight. Do you remember Sarah from our grade?"

"Yeah, I do," Billy said, searching for the face that matched the name.

"She just had a kid not too long ago and I told her I would go visit her."

"Well enjoy, Annie. I'll see you around," he said with a smile.

"Thanks for the mower," she replied, placing her arms on the truck window. A few raindrops began to hit the windshield as the two glanced outside in different directions, realizing that the rains were returning. Annie began to lean in a little to avoid the rain and their eyes met. She glanced down and looked over Billy's three-day-old beard, then lifted her eyes to meet his. He looked down at his keys and put them into the ignition, looking at Annie, who was now close and interested. He leaned in and felt his lips touch hers, slowly at first. The rains began to fall harder now and the two separated. She leaned over for one more quick kiss.

"Listen, I will see you later," Annie said as she started to walk backwards toward the house. Rain was beating against her mother's steel roof, her sweatshirt now half drenched.

"Yeah, see you later," Billy said as he started the truck and put in the clutch. Moving backwards, he watched as Annie walked toward the house. *Damn*, he thought, *she still looks fucking good in blue jeans.*

He changed the radio station, looking for something upbeat. Waylon Jennings found his way into the cab and Billy shook his head in approval as he drove, reinvigorated, down Main Street. Slapping his hands on the steering wheel, he pointed the old Ford toward his house.

"What to do, what to do," he muttered as he glanced out the window toward the distant hills. "Fucking beer tasted good!"

13

Sunday came early for Billy; typical Sunday morning, coffee and a shit, and then a drive to the café with Robert. Sunday morning breakfast generally lasted a few hours, with food and stories with the other locals. Some folks were just in for some homemade food, others a coffee stop after church. Billy and Robert had become Sunday regulars since Mother's passing. Before, it was time to time, but neither of them really wanted much but to be waited on.

It was also typical to rehab some of their gear on Sunday. Generally, basic rehab happened at the end of shifts, but once a week they would do a good cleaning of their gear. Robert and Billy would sharpen old chain, fix busted power-heads, and mix a lot of saw gas.

Billy paused from the sports page of the paper and pushed his plate aside. The biscuits and gravy were turning in his stomach, mixing with the numerous cups of coffee. He learned back in the booth, rubbing his stomach, smiling as the waitress came toward the table.

"Anything else, Billy? How about some pie?" she asked.

Robert lowered his paper to witness Billy's response. "Oh, no thank you, Mary, I'm full," Billy said, lifting the plate to hand to her.

Robert nodded in agreement and slid his plate toward her. "I'm full, too," he muttered and placed the paper down on the table. Taking another sip of coffee, he looked his son over. Billy glanced at his father and paused. "Hey, how about we go see Mom and Boone?"

Robert glanced out the window and nodded. "All right."

His dad did not say much as they left Main Street up a hill toward the town cemetery. Billy drove, content with the silence. His father gazed out the window and back at Billy. His kid did not really pick up on it, his mind appeared elsewhere.

"You know them corporate fuckers are gonna close Cadillac's mill down," Robert said as he reached for his can of chew.

"You hear more rumors about it?" Billy asked with some concern.

"Some guys been telling me that ever since everyone up there fought them on that dam, they were looking to get back at them."

"All I heard was that they were gonna drain the lake up there and blame it on the anglers," Billy said, yawning, rolling the window down to spit outside.

"I heard that too, but the head sonofabitch is from back east, staring at numbers, board feet and labor cost. He don't give a rat's ass about you or me, or any of them mill workers up there. I heard they were thinking about draining the lake, too."

"Amazing how we don't have any control over that," he said.

"Years back, this would not have happened, no way. Men would not put up with it." Robert shook his head. "Now, everyone making decisions has no damn fucking idea what they are doing, even the goddamn president! People are still building homes, wiping their asses, and now we are shipping logs off to Japan, for Christ sakes!"

Billy nodded in agreement as he parked the truck near their family gravesites. Robert opened the door and combed his hair with his hand, an attempt to look somewhat presentable for his buried boy and wife. Billy took his time walking to the gravesite. His father was already standing over his wife, staring at the standing stone by the time Billy joined him.

"They close the mill down, I'm libel to go crazy," Robert said, staring at his feet before kneeling down. Billy stood motionless, staring at his brother's tombstone, fighting the memory of his death. Billy nodded, though not really paying much mind to his father's comment.

"She was much stronger than I will ever be," Robert said, speaking softly, directing himself toward Billy. His son looked down on his father with his hands in his pockets, fighting the possibility of tears. Billy had no response as he watched his father struggle to pick himself up. Much of the recent weeks and months found countless minutes and hours in silence. Nether of them pushed or pried at each other. Both found comfort in work and drink, easy distractions. This was no different. Robert and Billy stood side by side, the last of the McDonough family in Polk County, staring over the rest of the McDonoughs. Robert kicked the soil beneath his boots and started gesturing toward the truck.

The two walked away, facing the town below them. The winds picked up their hair, tossing it around. Storm clouds were closing in on them, but neither paid much attention. It was just another damn day before a week of work. They climbed into the truck, slamming the doors in unison, still silent. The truck drifted its way back down the hill into town. Both looked at the tavern's parking lot, watching to see if they recognized any of the trucks parked in it.

"Looks like half the crew is down there today," Robert said. "We got any beer at the house?"

"Yeah, we got a few, but we should stop while we are here near the store," Billy said as he passed by the tavern and pulled into the store parking lot. He noticed Annie talking with her mom inside. Robert shook his head as he watched his son get more energetic. The two walked in and smiled and nodded toward Annie and her mother. Billy began heading in her direction while his old man aimed straight ahead for the beer.

"How are you two doing?" Billy asked, smiling at Annie.

"Good, Billy, "Annie said, her mother nodding with a grin before retreating to help customers.

"How was last night?" Billy asked, then nodded toward a logger who used to be on their crew.

"Good, she is good; baby is adorable," Annie said, running her eyes over Billy.

"Well, we are just in getting some supplies for the week," he said in response as his dad walked over with two cases of Pabst.

"I can see that," Annie said with a laugh.

Robert went up to the register to pay as Billy and Annie watched.

"Do you have a lot of work to do this week?" Annie asked, returning her attention to Billy.

"Yeah, kinda. I mean I should be busy until Saturday, n' maybe I will work Saturday, too. Hard tellin' not knowing," he said, casting his eyes towards her lips.

"Well, I'll be around if you want to hang out," Annie said, shrugging her shoulders.

"Yeah, that would be good. Stop by anytime. I'm usually at the bar or home by four or five," Billy said, noticing his dad leaving the store and heading toward the truck. "Listen, it would be good to catch up and actually spend some time bullshitting," he continued as he walked toward the door.

Annie agreed. "I'll see you - and be safe out there."

Billy nodded and smiled as he left the store, waving to her mother. He strutted toward the truck, where he found his dad in the driver's seat.

"Get in, lover boy," Robert shouted out the window, laughing.

Billy laughed and shook his head, reached for the door handle and slid in the seat. He reached for his ball cap and put it on. His dad was chuckling as they drove off. Billy turned his head toward the opposite traffic direction. "You're clear if you go now," he said to his dad.

"Okay then," Robert said as he pulled onto the street and headed home. The fire alarm bell was ringing, signaling it was noon. Every day, one of the volunteer firefighters would sound the alarm at noon to test it out. It was rather funny in a way, because afterward, one could hear several dogs throughout town howling their lungs out.

"Remember when they sounded that damn alarm for their tests, and Bill's fucking store was actually on fire," Robert said, laughing as he cracked a beer open for the drive home.

"Yeah, no one showed up, sorry fucker," Billy said as he watched the chief and a few others in front of the pumper.

The two men waived at the fireman. Robert honked his horn and smiled. The chief waved back, and then flipped Robert the fin-

ger. Robert and the chief had grown up together, though they were
not very close. They'd share drinks together at Ray's place. He had
tried to get the McDonoughs to volunteer for years, but without
much luck. Robert took his eyes off the station and glanced ahead
toward home. Billy kept quiet, hoping for a quick week.

14

The week was dragging for Billy, partly because he thought about Annie much of the time and partly because Robert was out there yelling at everyone. Most respected Robert and what he did and had done, but sometimes the constant orders got old. Billy would split the afternoons between home and the bar, waiting to see if her truck would pull up. Every time the tavern door opened, Billy would jerk his head, hoping to see her walk in. He was not much interested in talking shop after work that week, or shooting pool with the boys. He would either skip the afternoon drinks with the boys or keep them to a minimum. Going home actually appealed to him. He wanted the space in case she decided to come over.

Nothing much changed that week and Friday finally rolled around. Two of the log trucks went down for maintenance so the whole crew was not working Saturday. There was still some work to do that weekend, but Billy volunteered himself off. Others expressed interest in working, as many were broke from the unusually dry summer that left them in several fire precaution shutdowns. Billy and Robert were still comfortable with money. Billy also wanted to leave the possibility open for the weekend, something his father and some of the guys were starting to suspect.

Annie kept herself busy, volunteering at the small public library and traveling into the valley to shop. She drove around searching for jobs, but not trying too hard. She was still on a vacation, for all she thought. Everything in her life was just temporary.

So, the week was rather relaxing, cooking dinners for her mom and traveling along the rural Oregon roads.

She introduced herself to all her old teachers. Many of them were still there, dressed the same and preaching from the same textbooks and war stories. She walked through the hallways of the high school, often laughing at the pictures of people she used to know hanging on the aged walls. While in the library, she noticed a stack of yearbooks, and eagerly searched for the class of 1974. She examined the book, looking at the photos and quotes. She found a picture where she and Billy were coined best senior couple. She stared at the picture, smiling at the innocent look they gave the camera that day.

It was a major step back in time, but little seemed to have changed, both in the school and throughout the area. It was a far cry from the active life in the cities. Everything was slowing down for her that week. Billy was certainly a thought, but even though things were simple and slow, she felt busy with curiosity.

It was Friday, and she decided to visit another old friend who lived just east of town. She thought about Billy quite a bit that day, but she was not excited about having to deal with a bunch of screaming loggers that night. If this Friday was anything like last, then she was not really in the mood.

Billy parked himself at the bar and joined his crew for a cold one. A few beers later, Annie was a distant thought, as friendly pushes and billiard challenges were distracting his earlier wandering mind. Within no time, he was half drunk with the rest of the bar. Robert and most of the crew called it an early night. Some of them were going to work tomorrow, but Billy could care less. He and his high school buddy were still throwing back beers. Others would come and go, and friends would approach and speak, but Billy did not pay much mind. Cigarette after cigarette, beer after beer, the hours flew by.

Billy found some brief clarity in the bathroom, pissing all over the toilet seat and laughing to himself, slurring, "Fuck, I'm drunk!" Still laughing, he bounced off one of the walls before kicking the door open. His friend was having difficulty sitting on the bar stool and another guy was helping him stand up. Billy laughed as he composed himself and gave Ray a nod for another round. Ray shook his head and placed two bottles on the counter. "Your done after this, Billy" Ray said in a telling manner. Billy nodded in agreement and laid some cash down on the counter.

He took his beer and turned his back to his friend and Ray, then scanned the bar clientele. There were a few ladies in the bar that looked appealing to him, but some dudes accompanied them. The thought to go and talk to them ran through his mind, but quickly left. They looked good, but nothing worth throwing punches over. He tilted the beer back and finished it fast. He then slapped his hand down on the bar and began walking toward the door.

"You done, fucker?" his buddy slurred at Billy.

"Yeah," Billy said, smiling back, sending one last drunken glance at the ladies sitting nearby. "See you next time, brother," Billy shouted as he pushed the door open, causing him to open his eyes as he felt the brisk night air. "Fuck," he mumbled as he reached for his keys in his pocket. He walked up to the truck and opened the door, taking his time to get in and start the engine.

Annie quickly came into his mind, and he caught his breath and stared through the windshield into the darkness. "Just go home, idiot. No need to fuck that up just yet," he mumbled as he put the truck in gear. His world was beginning to spin and he found himself blinking hard to avoid it. The dark country road wove along, following the creek bed beside it. The truck often came close to the ditches, but all four tires stayed on the road. Before he knew it, he was at home falling onto his bed.

15

Hank crawled into bed, and nestled himself next to Billy. Robert had left some time ago for work and Hank was left for Billy to take care of. The dog was more or less self reliant, but needed some food and someone to occasionally open the door for him. Boredom had set in and Hank wanted some attention. He began to lick Billy and nudge at him with his nose. Billy lay still, not reacting to Hank's initial attempts. Hank responded with more force, nudged harder and moved around more in the bed. Billy began to move and roll over to slap the dog with a few friendly rubs. Hank got excited and jumped off the bed to the floor, chasing his tail in anticipation of Billy's rising. Billy threw one of his work socks out the door toward the living room. Hank's nails slid on the wooden floor as he darted toward the living room. Billy lifted his head, which felt swollen and heavy, and peered outside with one eye open to see the day that lay ahead.

It took him awhile to make it out into the kitchen. Hank was running around the living room and kitchen, excited to have Billy around for the day. Billy ignored Hank for the time being and searched for some coffee. Robert had been kind enough to leave a few cups in the pot for Billy. He poured a tall, dark cup and sipped it while holding himself up with one hand on the counter.

"Why do I keep doing this to myself?" Billy asked himself. He looked at Hank, expecting a response. Hank was trying his best to stay still, but his hunger and excitement were too much. He grabbed a bone nearby and began biting it. Billy smiled as he watched his friend keep himself busy.

"All right, you mutt, I'll feed you," Billy said as he sipped his coffee and looked for Hank's dog food.

This threw Hank into a restless fit of energy, tail wagging, stretching himself, eagerly anticipating Billy's throwing a few cups of dog food into his bowl. The second the food landed in the bowl, Hank began devouring it. Billy walked off smiling and debated whether he should return to bed or begin his day.

It appeared that someone was pulling down their driveway, judging by the sounds of rattling steel weaving its way over potholes and turns. Billy sipped his coffee and watched as Annie's truck pulled in and parked. He smiled, sipped another warm mouthful of coffee, and then leaned over a bit and smelled his armpit. "Jesus, you stink," he muttered, followed by a cough.

He continued to watch her as she turned the key off, flicked her hair and gave a quick glance in the rearview mirror. She got out of the truck and began walking toward the house. "God damn, she looks good today," he mumbled as he took another drink. She walked confidently, one foot guiding the other, old blue jeans and boots, a blouse that revealed her chest slightly. Blood rushed to his cheeks, a combination of caffeine and adrenaline. He snapped out of it, confused about what to do, smelled his armpit with disgust again, and ran toward his room. He wiped a quick strip of deodorant under his arm and put on his cleanest dirty shirt.

A gentle knock tapped against the front door. Billy rushed along the hardwood floors, sliding in his socks. He opened the door with a smile, their eyes met, and she began to smirk and raise her eyebrows.

"Come in," he said.

"Thanks," she said as she brushed past him.

He caught a whiff of her smell, which sent him thinking. "Want any coffee or anything?"

"Yeah, coffee sounds good," she said as she walked around the living room, staring at old photos. He brought her a cup and winced at the effects of his hangover. She held the cup with two hands, gazing outside at the creek.

"It's warm outside today," she said, returning her attention to Billy. He nodded, not aware of much except her. "Do you want to go for a walk up the falls where we used to swim?"

Billy nodded in agreement, amazed at how stupid and tired he felt. Of all the days she could choose to come over, she had to pick the one where he felt the worst.

"Yeah, it's been awhile since I hiked up there to the swimming hole," he said as he set down his cup and straightened his sore back. She watched and took notice to his fatigue. Billy grabbed his hat and began to put on some shoes for the hike.

Annie glanced around the house, "The house seems nice. Not sure what you were complaining about the other day."

"Nah, it's just a little empty. I moved back in once mom got sick."

Annie shook her head and set down her empty mug. She walked over to Billy and sat down next to him as he put on his shoes. He paused and looked at her, and she put her arms around his back and caressed him. "I'm so sorry for your loss, Billy. Your mom was a wonderful person, and Boone was always so fun to be around." Billy nodded as he squeezed her close, feeling her breasts against his chest. He let go, she did too, and she watched him tie his shoes. He rose, lost in thought, but ready to leave the house. Not saying much, he opened the door and looked back at Annie, who was staring at the floor.

"You ready?" Billy asked, and waited for her to lift her head.

"Yes," she said as she fought back tears.

They began their walk toward the falls, which were about a mile up the creek. The sun had found its way higher in the sky and shed its warm rays between the tall trees. Back in high school, the two of them used to hike around the creek and swim in its few deep swimming holes. They had first made love along the shores of the creek, just under the falls, but that was long ago, a distant memory.

That late morning the air was warm, but with just a bit of crispness from the gentle breeze. The summer was coming soon, and the spring scents and appearance of new growth and color were apparent. Springtime was Annie's favorite time of the year. It was a time of rebirth and change, the opening gates of sunshine and the departure of grayness that so often plagues the west side of the state for many bitter months. She pondered these thoughts and the way they reflected her current situation. This was her springtime, an escape from her winters, searching for some change with the sun.

The leaves looked healthy and green, and the creek's high water looked glossy and clean. The two hikers said nothing, simply walked and gazed at the tall trees and leftover stumps where the McDonough family had once logged. Occasionally, one of them would observe something or quickly note a forgotten memory, but for the most part, they walked in silence. But as time went on, Annie began to get bored with the quietness.

"I forgot how beautiful it is here," she said, slightly out of breath as she stopped along a rise in the trail.

Billy stopped behind her, nodding his head. "Well, why did you leave here in the first place?" he asked, knowing that it would change the conversation to something that had plagued him for many years now. He knew it was nice around here, no reason to talk about the pretty flowers and the creeks, the tall wooded hillsides and bushy understory. Though nearly a decade had passed, he was still a little bitter that she had left and never returned, or made any effort to communicate with him.

A brief moment of silence followed his question, long enough to hear each other's breath and the soothing sounds of the creek passing on by below them. "There were things that I wanted to do, like go to school and travel around," she finally said. "I regret the way I left and never looked back, but I think I needed to do that." She paused, nodded, satisfied with her answer, then scanned the landscape and brought her eyes back towards his.

"Was it worth it?" he replied as they walked further along the overgrown trail upstream.

"I think so. I met a bunch of nice people and I saw a lot of really nice places. There is a lot more to life than this town, this county, hell, even this state." She preached with her words and expressive hand movements. Billy knew better than to argue. He had traveled around a bit too, but this was his home and he was proud of it.

They trekked on and could hear the falls ahead in the distance. He walked behind her, often staring at her ass for motivation. He was lost and found entertainment in his perverted observation, watching as her ass cheeks parted from left to right with every step.

He smiled and chuckled. "What?" she asked as she slowed her stride.

"Nothing, nothing at all."

She did not believe him and assumed it was something crude. It usually was in his case, and time certainly did not cure him of that behavior.

They stopped on a ledge just downstream of the falls, whose mist collided with the sunshine. She sat on the rock, tilted her head back and enjoyed the sun's warmth, the mist cooling them down slightly. Billy ached as he sat down beside her. He grabbed a few rocks and threw them into the water. She waved her feet over the edge, waiting for him to look at her. He did, and she felt a little hopeless and vulnerable. He noticed, and moved in closer to kiss her. Their lips touched, softly at first, then with more energy. She separated herself, smiled and took off her boots, followed by her pants and blouse. Before long she stood up, naked and excited.

Billy sat surprised, then started to undress, stumbling over his boots, pants and shirt. She stood tall and firm; her breasts lay perfectly proportioned along her thin frame, hips providing small curves as he scanned her skin.

"Come on, hurry up. Let's go swimming," she said with a smile that reminded him of the past.

"Jesus, what got into you?" he shouted back laughing, his heavy head a mere thing of the past. So much for work and exercise to cure hangovers - naked women were the true medication. He slid off his underwear, causing her to give an approving grin. Billy stood tense and cold, causing him to flex his muscles and display his strength. Annie smiled and bumped him aside as she dove into the creek. She rose rather quickly, her body shooting out of the water long enough for Billy to see her erect nipples.

"Water's nice," she shouted at Billy, who stood just a few feet above her. She smiled as her lips began to shake a little from the cold.

"Oh shit," Billy mumbled as he dove into the water. Far from graceful, he hit the water hard and swam underneath until he rose just below the falls. Annie followed his lead, then flung her arms around his neck. Their bodies were tangled against each other as her legs wrapped around his wide frame, giving both of them a sense of much-needed warmth in the cold creek.

"I've been waiting for a real man," Annie said as she stared into Billy's eyes, preparing for a long kiss, short on breath, still shivering from the water.

"Well, I am not sure how real it's going to be, being that we're standing in cold fucking water," he said laughing. They began to kiss, grasping each other close, laughing momentarily before losing themselves in each other's arms.

"I want you," she mumbled as she grabbed his cock and massaged it a little. She rubbed him against her for awhile, trying to escape the coldness of the water, trying to escape the waters affect on their bodies. Billy moved closer and placed her gently against the rocks under the falls. She gasped after a few thrusts, not used to the feeling. She moaned and bit his shoulder a few times as Billy rocked back and forth, trying to keep his footing along the rocky bottom. The falls splashed water at them, beating gently against their exposed chests and backs. Pleasure battled with discomfort. Clumsiness guided their rhythms. They continued this act for several more minutes until they were overwhelmed with relief, causing them to pause and separate, gazing at each other, landing their lips again for a long kiss. Annie eventually pushed away leaving Billy alone near the falls.

She began to swim backwards under the falls and beyond, feeling the cool currents of the water tickle her body. Billy continued to stand below the falls for a while, admiring his lady swimming. He watched as she floated along the shallow waters of the swimming hole, then pushed off and swam toward her. He moved in quietly as she lay staring off into the sky, and picked her up and tossed her into the deeper waters. She retaliated by slapping the water with both hands to send it in his direction. He found it funny, because she couldn't send much water in his direction and her tits were bouncing around with each thrust of her hand.

His body was beginning to feel cold. His balls felt as if they had just been inverted inside his skin. He climbed out toward the rocks and lay down along the scattered clothes they had left behind. Reaching for his shirt, he found a pack of cigarettes and lit one up, lying down, breathing slowly. He slid into his underwear and looked into the sky. A few crows flew overhead, speaking nonsense in a piercing manner, and the treetops danced in rhythm with the ridge top winds. Annie had followed Billy out of the water, moved quickly, and cuddled next to Billy's wet, hairy chest.

"It's like we never grew any older," she whispered.

Billy smirked. "Yeah, but you were never that much of a freak," he said, laughing and coughing as he exhaled his smoke. She frowned and pinched his chest, but Billy was motionless.

"I just haven't had this good a time in a while," she said, sitting up and looking down at him.

"What, your old man didn't give you a good lay?"

"Not really. Not like this anyways."

"I see, so you are saying this was good?"

She smiled and looked down at Billy. "Yes, it was really good, and I am sure you like hearing that, too."

"Yeah, but I am used to hearing that," he returned with a smile, cigarette dangling from his lips, hands stretching above his head. Annie rolled over and tried to pin him down, but it did not last more than a few seconds before Billy rolled her back over and sat on top of her. He sat, back erect, taking one last drag from the cigarette, before handing it to her. She lay still topless, breasts hanging to their sides, nipples still hard and firm. Her other hand lay on her stomach just above his crotch. She exhaled and handed the cigarette back to Billy, who looked it over and put it out after taking a deep breath of air. He rose and helped pick her up. She began to put her blouse on as he fought with his pants. Within a few minutes they were dressed and ready to walk back. Billy noticed he was rather weak once they started walking, and realized it had been last night since he had eaten anything. Annie remained in a daze and walked with a smile as she followed Billy back to the house along the shores of the creek.

"You hungry?" Billy asked, speaking loudly from a few feet away.

"For what?" Annie replied with a curious tone, noticing her hunger with the question at hand.

"Not sure, but we have some grub at the house. I'll show you around the kitchen so you can get nice and comfortable there." He smiled and then laughed at his comment.

"You are such an asshole," she said as she trotted closer to him and jumped on his back. Her arms wrapped around his neck as Billy stumbled briefly to regain his footing in response to her surprise attack. He quickly adjusted and carried her for a while before she willingly released her grip and jumped off. A steady stream of smoke still drifted from the chimney, and Annie stopped to notice the scenic picture of the house as the cedar shingles painted a woodsy pattern against the forested backdrop. The house sat perfectly between the tall trees, and it was as if she had entered an old movie set. Billy did not think much of it, and headed in for some food.

16

Annie and Billy raided the refrigerator and were able to manage a few sandwiches and beers. The house was empty, and Annie found comfort eating her sandwich on the couch, reading the newspaper. Billy wolfed down his drink and food, sparking a lost energy, ready for the day with a new outlook that had started dim, but turned very bright. Billy walked toward the telephone and picked it up. This caused Annie to lower the pages long enough to cast a friendly smile at Billy, who did the same in return. He dialed the digits for Ray's Place.

The phone rang in the bar, where a few men sat drinking and bullshitting. Ray was away from the phone, so its rings echoed across the almost empty room.

"Well, it ain't for me. I don't know anyone who can remember seven numbers," a voice shouted as Ray picked up the phone. Robert chuckled at the man's response as he smoked his cigarette and reviewed some contracts.

"Robert, it's Billy," Ray said as he handed Robert the phone with a surprised look.

"What's wrong, boy?" Robert asked with some curiosity, wondering why his son was calling him at the bar.

"Nothing's wrong, Pops, just seeing what you were doing, thinking maybe I'd come down there if you were there."

"Okay then, why in the hell are you calling me? C'mon down then. Is that woman messing with your head?" Robert spoke loudly and much of the clientele in the bar could hear his end of the conversation.

Trying to pretend he was having a mature conversation with his dad, Billy continued to smile and nod as Annie watched Billy talk. She lay on the couch, finished reading the paper, entertained at the sight of her old friend. "Well, we are out of food here at the house."

Robert sat impatiently, listening to his kid act like an idiot. "Well then, go get some for Christ sakes!" He paused, then added, "Is she there with you now?"

"Yeah."

"Well, good for you. Glad to hear you ain't run her off yet. Why don't you come on down here and I'll show you some of these contracts I'm looking at. If we get some of these, we'll have plenty of work up until summer." Robert paused, waiting for a response.

"All right, I'll be down there in a bit," Billy said, waiting to hear his dad's response, but instead heard a click. He set the phone down and leaned back in the chair. Annie was waiting for something to be said. He smiled and looked her over. "You ready, babe?"

"Oh, so it's babe now?" Annie spoke, raising her eyebrows, perking her chest in an attempt to stand her ground. Billy stood up and Annie did the same. She moved close, wrapping her arms around his shoulders. He kissed her on the neck and picked her up, forcing her legs around his waist. He walked toward his room, her legs dangling at times as she reacted to kisses and movement.

They stopped at the edge of the bed where he laid her down gently. She separated herself long enough to quickly undress, and Billy did the same. She hesitated, the feeling of uncertainty soon passed as the two rolled around as he tickled her insides. She let out enjoyable gasps with each thrust. Sweat began to bead on his forehead as he moved to an unconscious sounds of her moans and noises from the bed.

She had been unfulfilled and overdue, and he soon made up for her emptiness. Minutes passed, and eventually Billy rolled off Annie, who lay still, smiling, riding the wave of pleasure. She had difficulty breathing. She trembled for a brief moment, wiping tears with laughs. Billy smiled, then reached for a cigarette. He rose up and began dressing himself, wordless, cigarette dangling from his lips, squinting to avoid smoke in his eyes. Annie watched, content with laying down, slowly recovering with a smile.

"All right, let's get going," Billy said as he sat to put on his shoes, cigarette dangling as he talked.

Annie rolled over, her ass fully exposed, face tilted slightly, and began to sweetly whine, "Let's stay in. I can cook you dinner tonight. Let's just lay around and be lazy."

"Nah, fuck it. Let's get going. I have to look over a few things."

"All right," she said, somewhat disappointed, but slowly began to dress herself. Billy was, amused but slightly impatient as he watched Annie take her time getting dressed. They eventually made their way outside where the day had passed them by faster than expected. Dusk was making its appearance with a few distant stars in the sky and a hint of darkness in the light. They hopped in the truck, gave each other a quick smile, and began driving toward town. Annie gazed out at the forest, then up toward the sky, searching for the early stars.

"I always loved astronomy, but there was just too much math involved with it," she said as her eyes searched for the first stars of the night.

Billy nodded, smiled and returned the observation with, "I always loved the math and hated the astronomy part of it."

Annie looked at Billy with a fair amount of disgust, folding her arms. "Fine. I'll shut up." Billy smiled and acknowledged her statement. He focused on the road and kept his eyes out for deer. She sat, somewhat content yet frustrated. Not until now did she have the time to look back on the day and contemplate what was happening. She fought with clarity and rational thoughts, tried to relax and enjoy the time she had, occasionally looking over at Billy to see his concentration on the road and other things, wondering what or where his thoughts were. She glanced over the truck, not initially noticing its wear and tear, its dirt and stink, and realizing that as she had left her truck at his house, she was somewhat dependent on Billy.

17

The bar was almost empty, with about a half dozen trucks lining the parking lot. It was early, but it was still slower than a typical day. The two got out of the truck and walked toward the entrance. Billy walked in first, where the clientele properly greeted him. "Oh shit, look what the cat dragged in," yelled someone at the end of the bar, followed by another, "Oh fuck."

Billy ignored much of the harassment with smiles and nothing more. The sarcasm subsided once they realized Annie followed him. No one in there knew her from anyone else, and they gave her friendly stares and nods.

Robert sat in the back of the bar, surrounded by paperwork, empty glasses and ashtrays. "What happened, you take the fucking scenic route?" Billy smiled and ignored the question as he signaled a drink order to Ray. They sat down; Annie interested in the paperwork and Robert's concerns.

"It's all just some legal shit," Robert mumbled at Annie as a way to greet her.

"Well, I am a lawyer," she responded, smiling as she peeked at some of the contracts and bank statements. Robert took off his reading glasses and looked at Billy with puzzlement, then looked at Annie. "Bullshit."

"Really, I am. I mean I'm licensed in the State of Washington. Technically, I can't practice in Oregon yet. What are you working on?" she asked with a smile. Robert was taken aback. Most of the lawyers he knew were slime balls; guys in suits and oozing of greed and need, taking, never giving, speaking, never listening. He was puzzled and said, "Oh Jesus, a little of everything. Looking over some cutting unit contracts, things with the mill in Cadillac and others in Creekville, and some bank loans."

"All right, I can certainly look it over for you if you'd like," she said, looking at Robert, genuinely interested. Robert rocked back against the chair and nodded with a smile.

"That would be nice if you could." He studied her face as she moved her head in response to the different pages. He glanced over at Billy, who got up and walked toward the bar for another round. "Hey, kid, did you know she was a damn lawyer?"

"Nope," Billy responded. He had heard that before, but did not pay it much mind. He stood erect, content with his day, waiting for Ray to return with some drinks, oblivious of the other folks in the bar.

"Hey, Billy," a voice called out from the end of the bar.

"Oh shit, how are you doing, Robbie?"

"Not bad at all."

Robbie was a soft-spoken man from New York, a college-educated draft dodger. He'd moved out west about 12 years before with his wife, and accidentally ended up in Hemlock. He briefly worked in the woods before he stumbled into a maintenance job for the county. He had grown comfortable in Hemlock and called it home. Most of the town's longtime locals considered him one of them. Billy and Robbie would spend hours talking about sports, music and books. Too many times, the two would get drunk together, laughing about something of little or no importance. Oftentimes, Robbie's wife would have to come down to the bar and drag him away.

Billy and Robbie collided with a handshake and smile as Robbie whispered rather loudly, "You get some pussy? Hell, you are all full of smiles." Robbie took his eyes off Billy and glanced down the bar at Annie.

"I may have," Billy said, smiling as he studied his whiskey glass.

"Get over here, boy!" Robert yelled from across the bar. Billy nodded in his father's direction and cut his conversation with Robbie to an end. The whiskey had a slight burn in his throat and a gentle ease to his head. He rubbed his shoulder as he approached his father and Annie. She perked up and noticed him massaging his shoulder. There was not much pain, just a general tiredness to his joints.

"I'm thinking about buying some acres just on the other side of the range there in Lincoln County. There's some good fir and cedar there, and cedar is still bringing in high dollar," Robert explained to his son, who nodded in agreement. The McDonoughs were somewhat unusual in their logging habits. They owned a fair amount of land and equipment, even though most of their work came from contracts from large-scale logging companies.

"The mill in Creekville is laying off a bunch of men, so it would be a further turnaround for cedar trees now…and who knows what's going to happen up in Cadillac. I guess Columbia Logging is going to have a town hall meeting next week to lay out their game plan, probably lose a lot of jobs." Robert shook his head and grabbed a cigarette from his shirt pocket, coughing as he searched for matches. Billy reached into his pocket and handed some to Robert, who nodded in thanks.

Robert continued, "They have logged about 90 percent of the land they owned around Cadillac. Since heading to a plywood mill, the trees are smaller and the land is growing thin for them. I just don't see them staying open."

Annie watched the two men briefly ponder. She, too, was concerned. "Are the board feet and smaller trees the only thing?"

Billy looked up at Robert, who smirked, responding, "Well, there is the issue of a dam that no one can agree on."

"What is up with that?" she continued on.

"There are rumors of them draining the lake up there if they don't get their way. There are rumors that the wood they are putting out ain't cutting it; too many mills too close, not enough board feet needed." Robert paused to inhale his cigarette, taking a long drag. "I have not heard it this bad ever. If that mill…if that town makes it through the winter, I would be shocked."

The three sat silent, all thinking the same thing. If the mill closed in Cadillac, then business as usual would change drastically for them. Longer commutes to mills elsewhere would be inevitable. Their equipment was old and their turnarounds for their trucks were generally pretty quick with the mill just up the road. They owned some land, but used it as a last resort, not enough to sustain work year round. If the mill closed, competition would immediately increase and contracts would be a low-balling affair. Columbia Logging owned all the land within the town and its surroundings, except a small, 120-acre parcel the McDonoughs owned bordering the town and mill. Throughout the last several years, Columbia Logging and its predecessors had tried to buy them out, but the family's stubborn ways always avoided the pressure. They logged some of it, but left most of the timber as an untouched stand waiting for hard days.

There were only a few small logging outfits in the western part of the county. Because of the farms that stretched to the east, much of the other logging outfits worked dozens of miles to the north and south, and the mills were a better part of 50 miles from that. Geographically, their corner of the world was prime, but the rumors of Cadillac and even Creekville closing down would bring certain harder times for the McDonoughs and other logging outfits.

Their crew had a fair amount of work that would keep them steady up into summer. Robert had a paranoid approach to his work, which oftentimes was far from reality, but times were changing. More mills were closing around the state at a faster pace, and new environmental concerns were hot topics in the news. Small outfits were beginning to cave to larger companies. Columbia Logging Company was just another player in the game, dictating people's lives with the stroke of a pen.

Billy glanced at Annie and the two exchanged smiles. He could tell she was bored, and wanted to leave. Robert excused himself and went to the bathroom. Billy whispered to Annie, "You want to get out of here?"

Annie smiled and nodded in approval. The two rose from their chairs as Billy grabbed his glass and finished the remaining beer in two large gulps, followed by an impressive belch. The two walked out of the bar as Billy nodded and threw out a few handshakes at fellow drinkers. "I'll see you later," Billy said in passing to Robbie as he slapped him on the shoulder.

"Okay, Billy, you take care and be safe," Robbie gestured as he perked up from his book with a smile. Robert had returned to his table and watched his boy leave the bar with Annie. He smiled and shook his head, muttering, "Wonder if I'm going to get any work out of him anymore?"

Billy reached out his hand and placed it as gently as he could on the back of Annie's neck. She caved in and reached her arms around his side. She was glad to leave the bar. It depressed her, seeing the sad and lonely faces escaping something in the dark confines of its smoky walls. Billy opened the truck door for Annie, then jumped in and straightened his back as he turned the key. The truck coughed a bit as he reached for a gear. Annie studied him momentarily.

"Do you like living with your dad?"

Billy was a little taken back by the question and gazed out the window to look for oncoming traffic. Looking over at Annie, he said, "It's okay. I mean, he ain't around much." Pausing, looking down the road at the approaching store, he said, "I had a place just up here off of Washington Street for a few years, but gave it up when Ma got sick."

Annie nodded and watched the houses go by, one by one. Billy dipped off the road into the gravel parking lot of the store. He jumped out of the truck and gazed back at Annie. "You want anything?" She shook her head, declining, watching as Billy walked into the store. She rested her head against the seat and pondered the day, what had happened and what it might still bring. "What am I doing?" she muttered as she looked into the sky for the stars. The clouds sent a mosaic of layers blocking any continuity in the patterns of the sky, but patches of clearness presented some beams of far-off lights.

Billy returned, interrupting her daydreams and concerns, and tossed a case of beer between the two of them with a loaf of bread and some jelly. Annie smirked at the purchase as he shot quickly back in reverse. He pointed the old mule toward the dark, deserted road back home. The turns of the winding road relaxed Annie, who closed her eyes and napped as Billy kept quiet. The truck found its way to the driveway, where Hank greeted them with a few barks and a wagging tail. The truck stopped and Annie opened her eyes to a dark house. Hank jumped into the truck to lick and greet Annie, who wrestled free of the welcoming retriever with smiles and laughs.

The house was dark and cold. Billy stumbled for a light switch. There was a calming effect to the house, even when cold, that Annie loved. Far from the streetlights and sirens of the city apartment she was used to. Far from the marble and crystal that seemed so long ago. The living room had a simple layout: a few chairs and a couch surrounding a small stove and TV. Billy began chopping kindling and placed the small pieces of wood systematically over his crushed newspaper. A crackling fire appeared seconds later and he rose from his kneeling position, looking at Annie. "It will get warm in here in a minute."

She smiled and watched as Hank searched for a toy. "Is he hungry?" she asked, entertained as the dog chased his tail.

"Oh, probably," Billy said as he took off his shoes. Annie walked into the small kitchen that aligned the living room. She grabbed a cup and scooped a few mounds of food into Hank's dog bowl. He wagged his tail and gave Annie a thankful nod. She smiled and glanced over the worn-down kitchen. She walked around the house looking at the old logging and family photos, smiling at the pictures of Billy as a young kid.

She looked down at Billy, who tried to read the titles of the albums. "Can I have a beer?"

He paused. "Of course. Grab me one, too."

Annie nodded. "What's for dinner?" she asked, looking at the bread and jelly.

"Not sure; there is always pb n' j's."

Annie smiled and shook her head. "I need to go shopping so that I can cook you guys a real meal." Billy nodded and put on a jazz record.

"I didn't know you liked jazz?" Annie said as she opened her beer, puzzled but amused. "Yeah, it's okay. You surprised?" She was taken aback.

"A little, I guess. I thought you just liked country and rock and roll."

Billy smiled. "I like most music. You know, us backwoods folks ain't as sheltered as you may think."

Annie laughed, raised her can of Olympia and pointed it toward Billy. "You could have fooled me."

Billy smirked and sat down in a chair near the fire across from Annie. Their eyes met, long enough for them to pause, think and wonder. She broke away, not wanting to face the reality of today. Billy finished his beer and got up to grab another, then returned to his seat and put another log on the fire.

Annie began to go on a friendly rant about all the places she had seen and all the people she met at college and in Seattle. She talked about how great it was studying back east and seeing the history and changes in the landscape of different places. She briefly would bring up her ex, as if by accident, with stories of travel and Seattle. She talked about her law firm in Seattle and how she began to see the greed and fakeness that plagued so many of her colleagues. Her excitement to practice law suddenly became irritating.

Billy sat silent, not saying much, feeding the conversation when it went silent. He did not want to talk much about the last decade, or the recent death of his mother and brother. Instead, she went on about her trips to Europe and Mexico, and how she loved to travel and try new things. Billy had not left the state much over the past several years. He went to Canada twice, once for work felling large trees on a wildfire, and once for a quick trip with a few buddies. He drove across country to see his older brother in New York, but much of the last decade was spent living and working around Hemlock. He had a curiosity of other places and the thought of tropical beaches always sounded appealing, but work and life in Hemlock kept him in.

After hours of conversation, Annie was finally showing her fatigue. She finished her last sip of beer, gazing at Billy, who was awaiting another story to guide him deeper into the night. Annie smiled at Billy as she set down her empty can. "Take me to bed."

Billy smiled, thankful that her stories were halting for the time being. He picked himself up and set down his empty can, then walked to Annie and reached down and picked her up with ease. She smiled with surprise and wrapped her arms around his neck as she watched ahead, pointing out tripping hazards to Billy, who was limited on visibility. They found the bed, where Billy laid her down. She smiled and watched as Billy took off his shirt and pants, pausing before taking his underwear and socks off. He stood naked as she began taking her clothes off. The bed was still a mess from earlier. The lamp was on its side and a few pictures had fallen off the shelves. Billy picked up the lamp and placed it upright as Annie lay naked and still in the room. The moonlight placed enough light to make out her small nipples and wavy hips. Little goose bumps scattered across her cold skin. Billy lay down and threw some covers over the two of them.

She moved in, resting her head against his chest, her arm and leg lying across his body. He stared at the wall, tired from a long day and endless conversation, beer and its effects throughout the last several days. She kissed his chest and began dragging her hand gently across his stomach, lowering it closer and closer to his cock. He lay still, amused, but tired. She moved her hand back up to his stomach and massaged it with a gentle touch. He began breathing more deeply as she tilted her head and kissed him on the lips. She moved her head back to his chest as he broke out in a few quiet snores. She smiled and lay still, eventually closing her eyes and dreaming.

18

Annie awoke to a cool breeze that seeped through the partially opened window. Seconds later, she rolled over and looked outside to see Robert and Billy talking and chopping wood. Hank was running around with an oversized, freshly-cut piece of wood, which dangled from his growling mouth as he begged for attention. Annie chuckled as she watched the dog run around in circles. She tried to wipe the sleep from her eyes and struggled to leave the warm confines of the bed. Billy had set a cup of coffee on the nightstand for her. She smiled and took a sip, and quickly spit the cold coffee back in the cup. The coffee had been there awhile. She laughed at herself after a moment of disgust.

Her underwear lay across the floor; she walked over and put it on. She noticed one of Billy's shirts lying on the nearby chair, walked over and put it on. The shirt draped around over her like a short skirt and smelled faintly of gasoline, smoke and body odor. Normally, these smells would annoy her, but today she did not mind. Annie opened the bedroom door and headed for the kitchen to pour herself a warm cup of coffee, then headed to the bathroom. It smelled faintly, dissipated a bit by a burning candle. An ashtray lay beside the sink with a lingering coat of spit and toothpaste. She headed to the back door to greet Billy and Robert.

"Good morning," Annie said as she rested both hands on the warm coffee mug and leaned against the doorframe. Her back felt the remaining warmth of the morning fire in the stove, her chest slowly feeling the cooling effects of the morning breeze.

Robert turned at the greeting, then smiled and nodded. He was taken aback at Annie's beauty and smile. Billy grinned at her and set down the splitting maul, amazed at her appearance. Even Hank stopped running around to take a peek.

"How are you feeling, babe?" Billy said as he paused to wipe sweat from his forehead.

"Great, I slept well," she shouted back, staring at him, enjoying another warm sip. She walked closer to the two men before realizing that even with the morning sun and warm coffee, it was still chilly outside. "Who wants breakfast?"

Billy said quickly, "That would be great." The two men smiled at each other as they watched her walk briskly back into the house.

Robert grabbed the back of Billy's neck and shook it. "Now don't go and fuck this one up." He laughed at his thoughts and took a seat at the edge of the deck, looking up at Billy while lighting a smoke. Hank ran toward him with his stick and begged for a toss. Robert smiled, grabbed the stick from the dog and faked throwing one way, but the old dog was smarter than to take the bait. He barked and asked for a real toss. Robert stood up and launched the stick deep into the brushy understory.

"She's a good one, ain't she?" Billy said as he sent the maul violently through a piece of alder. The alder was invading many of the fir stands, usually along the creeks and rivers. Often they would take it home and burn it or give it away to friends for firewood. Many of the piles of wood they cut were mixed species. Robert liked to burn oak for its hard, lengthy burn period. Robert got up and placed a piece of cherry on the block for Billy, who swung the maul back, but brought it down sideways on the piece. He quickly regained composure and sent the piece in separate directions.

"I figure we should run Ray a load of wood; been a few months since we last did that."

"Sure thing. Maybe I'll run it over to him sometime this week," Billy said as he stopped again to wipe the sweat that began to drip down his face.

Giving away firewood was a common action of the McDonoughs. Either as paybacks, loans, trades, or gifts, they would often fill up their trucks and drop a load of cut wood at friends' places. It was a benefit for all involved. They rarely paid for meat, as they would drop off several cords a year to the town's butcher in exchange for good cuts of meat. Ray would often only accept payment on half the drinks they ordered at the bar, which even at that rate kept him open. It did not take much effort for Billy and Robert to chop a few cords for folks. Many of the residents of Hemlock heated their homes with wood, so an extra cord here and there was a much-appreciated gesture.

Annie had made do with what was available in the kitchen. Luckily, breakfast foods were always around. She sliced some potatoes and began frying them in the cast iron pan, and balanced her time cooking bacon and a few eggs. She was able to create a favorite of any egg and bacon lover, as large mounds of potatoes and bacon crowded each plate, followed by pieces of toast and eggs on top. She opened the window and shouted at the two, "Breakfast is served!"

Billy and Robert rushed to the house like two little kids on Christmas morning. The sat down, full of smiles, glanced at the food, and devoured it in a matter of minutes. Billy sat back in his chair, catching his breath, as Robert burped and reached for a smoke. Annie shook her head, still cleaning up some of her egg with the remaining toast. "That was damn good, damn good, Annie," Robert said as he watched Annie dab at her mouth with a napkin. Billy shook his head in agreement.

"Thank you," she smiled and grabbed the empty plates.

After she washed the dishes, she found Billy on the couch reading the Sunday paper. She sat next to him with a fresh cup of coffee. She quickly turned to the paper and began reading. After examining much of it, she saw Billy beside her taking a nap, recovering from their late breakfast. She smiled and began watching him, listening to Robert snore from his back bedroom. Hank had found comfort at her feet, and she looked outside to the passing stream near the house, the tall trees dancing around a bit in the breeze.

Moments later, she quietly picked herself up and walked toward Billy's room to find her truck keys. He heard her get up and followed her to the room. She did not notice as he stood in the doorway, curiously watching her pick through his clothes and things. Turning back toward the door, she jumped slightly once she realized Billy had been watching. "What are you doing?" he asked, leaning an arm against the doorway.

"Looking for my keys. I should get going and leave you be."

Billy nodded and hesitated before speaking. "Did you leave them in your truck?" Annie smiled at Billy. "Probably."

She walked over to Billy and stared deeply in his eyes, "Thank you," she whispered as she landed a wet kiss on his lips. He returned the favor and gently pushed her toward the bed. She hesitated briefly before allowing him to guide her. They lay down without words, just breaths and thoughts, touch and smell, wonders and grins. She raised her arms and wrapped them around his back as he peppered her neck with soft kisses. He rolled over and she sat on top of him and looked down. "I have to go, Billy." He nodded again and raised his arms, resting them behind his neck. They stared again at each other, smiling, so many days in between 10 years, so many others that treated themselves with each other, so many stories and secrets unrevealed. All meaningless, all other worries sent packing with the wind.

Annie got off him and helped him out of bed. They walked outside toward her truck, where he opened the door and looked in to find the keys still in the ignition. He smiled and pointed at the keys. She shook her head and got in the truck. He shut the door for her and rested his arms on her window frame. "I will try and see you tomorrow," she said in a very relaxed quiet tone.

Billy responded, "Well, I will probably be in one of two places," as he pushed himself off the window and walked off. She started the truck and looked out the back window as she pulled away, seeing the house where Billy stood and gave her a wave. She smiled and waved back.

Billy entered the house and headed toward the kitchen for a beer. Robert had just taken a sip from his beer and walked into the living room, cutting a fart. Billy broke into childish laughter, holding himself up with one hand on the sink, dipping his head, spilling the beer,

"Nice entry," Billy said, wiping his mouth.

Robert chuckled. "Where's Annie?"

Billy stopped laughing and his face changed into a serious look. "She's gone home to hang out with her mom."

Robert sat down on the couch and looked at Billy, who still stood against the sink. "Are we ready for work tomorrow?"

"Gear's in the truck," Billy said as he finished his beer and set the can down.

"Okay then, I'm going to head out there with you tomorrow. Figure I can do something else but read paperwork and annoy Ray." Robert still looked his son over as he watched Billy open another beer and look back. "Sure you're ready for work tomorrow?" Billy smiled at his dad and nodded.

19

It was half past five when Billy and Robert left their home and headed down the road in Billy's truck. Hank had hitched a ride and lay motionless between the two men. The sun had not quite reached over the distant Cascades.

Robert always drove when the two of them went somewhere, and it drove Billy nuts. Both were control freaks that constantly corrected each other's driving habits. The Ford truck wove its way along several windy roads until they approached Red's place. Red was standing outside in the cold, smoking a cigarette, and impatiently awaiting his normal commute with Billy.

"Well, you boys are late this morning," Red griped as he waiting for Hank to get in the bed of the truck, grunting at the fact that he was traveling with three versus the normal two.

"You know Dad; he had to do his makeup this morning," Billy said. Robert lit a cigarette and ignored the complaints, sending the truck in a quick reverse.

The three men did not talk all that much as the truck hit every bump along the switchback roads, some cutting through overgrown re-growth stands, some of the road hung balancing along steep slopes. They approached a wide spot in the road where they saw some familiar trucks just a half-mile from the landing; their crew circled up sipping coffee, sucking down cigarettes and spitting their chew. The Ford truck came to an angry halt. Everyone knew who was driving and prepared for it. "What's the deal, boys?" Robert said as he rolled down the window, wide-eyed and disgruntled.

"Fucking hippies are camped out in the road just around the bend," one of the choker boys said with a smirk.

"God damn it!" Robert screamed as he pulled up the road toward the landing. They skidded a few dozen yards short of a couple vans and tents that sat blocking the road. A miserable attempt for a warming fire was sending whiffs of wet smoke into the air as two long-haired men and one short-haired woman walked casually about.

Robert lit a cigarette and laid his hand on the horn for several long seconds. This caused people to rise out of their tents and without much practice or routine, form a line across the narrow road. He took a long drag from his cigarette and ran his hand through his thinning hair, trying to calm his nerves. "Jesus Christ, I am going to kill them all," he said shaking his head. Red was smirking, thinking the same thing.

Billy just shook his head in amazement. "Billy, will you go get them out of the way?" Robert asked, looking at Billy with an impatient stare.

"Just what my morning needs," Billy muttered under his breath.

Billy opened the passenger door and robbed Red of one of his smokes, lit it and exhaled outside as he stepped from the truck. He slowly walked toward the small crowd, focused in on the prettiest girl, looked her briefly over, smiled and kindly asked, "How is the camping trip?"

"I don't talk to tree killers!" she shouted back, looking down the line at her friends, receiving claps and praises for her response. Billy chuckled in response, glanced over the crowd and took a long drag from his cigarette. He looked back at the truck where Red and Robert sat staring, muttering words that he could only guess about.

"All right, folks, listen up and listen good. My family owns this land. We even paid a guy to build this here road. We are a small outfit that does not make much money or even cut that much wood. If you want to make a difference, go picket some large corporate son-of-a-bitch or stand in an entrance to some mill." Billy paused, took another drag, not ready for this wake-up to a long day. He grew angry and impatient.

"Hell no, we won't go!" shouted one of the young men, and the rest chimed in.

Billy smiled and raised his head. "Listen, we can do this the hard way or the easy way, but either way we are driving up this road. My father hates tree huggers, hates them more than the Russians, and he is good friends with the sheriff." Billy paused and looked each one in the eye, took another drag from his smoke and continued, "So, if I was you, I'd take your college asses back home and leave while you can." Billy stopped talking and took a step back, tossing his cigarette to the ground. The protesters stood silent momentarily, contemplating their immediate future, before one piped up, "Fuck you, man."

"Fuck!" Robert shouted from inside the cab, then opened the door, cigarette dangling from his mouth. He pushed the seat forward and grabbed the hunting rifle, cocking the lever action as he moved away from the truck. "Out of the way, boy," Robert yelled at Billy, who had already started walking back toward the truck. Robert fired a round at a nearby tree and the shot echoed across neighboring canyons. The line dropped to their knees as they covered their ears in response.

"Get off my land before I bury every one of you faggots!" Robert shouted as he cocked in another round. The crowd was uneasy and weary, eyes glancing from one to another, full of fear. A girl cried from the distance, "You are going to kill all these trees."

"Probably so, " Robert said as he took his last drag from his cigarette and flicked it in their direction, "and when I am done, you can wipe your fucking tears on some Kleenex, wipe your pretty lil' ass on some toilet paper, and write down how much you hate me on some fucking paper!"

Robert was angry, his veins popping from his neck and forehead, and the young girl who'd recently piped up sat with her head between her legs, sobbing. Robert breathed fast and deep, waiting for a move, waiting for an excuse to use as an example.

Billy watched from the truck, leaning against the open door, arms resting on the window frame. He stood thinking, trying to find who was actually right and wrong. They were trespassing, but may have had a point. However, a man needs to let another man work and provide. Both sides had their reasons; some of those reasons made sense, and some of them were just opinions based on nonsense and ignorance. These folks never really bothered Billy very much the way they did his dad. They never existed in his father's generation. Loggers were seen as heroes, like veterans and firemen, but nowadays, if you cut a tree, you were scorned. Most folks who hate loggers never dropped a tree. Never looked up at one, hugged it, judged its lean, tapped its bark and talked with it. Once they set a saw in a standing tree and watched it fall... it's hard to be against it. Once they stumbled to move away as the holding wood barked and cracked, watching with one eye on the tree, the other on their escape. Once they'd realized they opened up the canopy and lived another day to talk about it, things change. No one wanted to see every tree be cut, well maybe, besides Red, but most folks, even loggers, know that you have to manage the lands.

Seconds passed and the morning silence lingered. Robert pointed at a boy who stood below a tree. He shouted at the innocent-looking young man, "You even know what kind of tree that is?"

The boy took a step back and shouted, "It's a cedar?"

"Jesus Christ! It's a goddamn fir tree, son. If you are willing to fight for something, at least know what you are fighting for. Look at the bark, Jesus Christ! Look at the branches, son!" Robert began to pace, looking over the frightened faces, his rifle lying over his shoulder. "Now hurry up and get out of here!" he griped again, looking like a drill sergeant in the army, pacing back and forth pointing and yelling.

The group got up as Robert stopped pacing and lit another cigarette. He walked back to the truck and leaned against it, letting his rifle sit against his hip, pointed toward the sky. The hippies began tearing down their camp, picking up trash and stomping out their sorry attempt at a fire. Many of the girls were crying and the men walked with their heads hanging low. Robert stood motionless as he studied their every move, desperately looking for something else to correct them on. Billy had found his seat back in the truck where Red chuckled at the show. Robert walked toward his seat and placed the gun behind it. He smirked, "Goddamn hippies." He reached for the handle to help him into the seat while the vans were leaving the human blockade and heading back down the hill.

"I bet one of them actually shit their pants," Red said, laughing and shaking his head.

"I just don't get it anymore," Robert mumbled as he scanned the landscape.

Robert was still upset. The crew was getting a paid break for the show. He started the truck again and continued up the hill until they got to the landing where the loader stood. He began to mumble as Red and Billy stood silent. "Jesus, those kids didn't even have a clue what kind of tree they were trying to save…if you are going to fight a war, might be a good idea to know the enemy." He parked the truck out of the way against some brush and picked up the CB radio. "All right, boys, let's get to work."

20

Billy and Red hopped out of the passenger seat into the thick underbrush where Robert had parked. They looked at each other. The fact that it was early and Monday was bad enough, not to mention Robert was on scene, and his parking habits to top it off. They struggled through the brush to the bed of the truck and gazed up the ridge at an area they were going to clear. Inspecting their gear and saws, both paused and began putting an edge on their saw chain. Hank lay down inside the bed with his head resting on his paws and watched, inspecting their sharpening capabilities. The dog often followed Billy and Red around as they dropped trees. He did a good job of staying out of the fall, and would run around on top of the fallen trees, jumping from one to the other.

Robert lit another cigarette as he paced around his equipment and the landing. The three trucks that had been waiting for the hippies to descend had finally appeared. The men took their time eyeing Robert with disdain, crawling from their seats, some stretching, and some waiting to be briefed. Some of the folks walked toward their duties, others stood gazing with tired eyes at another Monday.

"I wanna see bruises on your arms," Robert yelled at the choker boys. They nodded without a response and headed down the slope to where Billy and Red had laid down a few acres of trees just a week ago. Robert watched as his crew scattered around in various directions and began work. He stared at the tower and its few cables that stretched far off in the distance, evaluating their positioning. Walking slowly back to the truck, he looked over the land and roads that Lee's construction crew had put in. Nodding his head in approval, he rested his leg on the truck's tire and began double knotting his boots.

"Here you go, Dad," Billy said as he handed his father his saw, sharp and ready, full of oil and gas. The yarder's diesel engine started, causing both Robert and Billy to look at each other for a brief moment, stone faced and silent. Robert nodded at Billy and grabbed his saw, looking it over as he marched closer to the landing's logs. He rested the bar over a log and fired it up. After two pulls on the choke, it started and he began limbing some of the leftover timber. Robert would sometimes limb and flush cut stumps that got in the way of the lines and dragging trees, but most of the time he patrolled various cutting sites and did paperwork, worked on the equipment, and yelled at his workers.

Billy and Red hopped back in the truck and drove a few hundred yards up the road to their next logging site. Robert did not much notice as he skipped around the logs, limbing them and measuring their length and size, prepping them for a load to the mill. Still excited to see them head off the hill toward the mill, heading to who knows where from there. The hours in the tavern hiding from sweat and work, always plagued Robert in ways that were not noticeable until he got with his crew in the middle of it. The beer tasted better when the day found sweat and a little pain. He was thankful for the work again. His hands needed the distraction; his mind needed to wander.

If the logs were not already waiting on the hill whenever Robert was around, the crew generally pumped out another load. Everyone knew that. No one on the crew was lazy or content with just a few to a dozen loads; their crew was strong and experienced. They did not accept usual loads. It was not uncommon to see 18 to 20 loads a day come off their hills. If the numbers were down, there was generally a good reason other than laziness or stupidity.

Midday hit fast, and the men rested their tired, rugged bodies on stumps and logs and began eating their lunch. One man laid down the whistle punk for a long time, giving the notion for a lunch break. Robert nodded at the men and began to slowly walk up the ridge toward Billy and Red. With the equipment shut down and everyone quiet, Robert could hear the two fallers yelling at each other from a distance, trying his best though half deaf, and trying to ignore his own footsteps and breaths as he marched on.

Seconds after noticing Billy among the tall brush and the remaining trees, Robert sat down on dead log and watched his son tear through the bark and into the heart of the tree. He was proud of his son. Billy was dedicated and intelligent when it came to logging. He worked hard, and everyone knew that. Robert made it hard for him to prove himself, and there was not one soul on the crew, past or present, who ever questioned Billy's dedication or craft.

Robert watched as the fir tree dropped side slope and crashed along the hillside. Billy gave Red a yell and Red began cutting his tree cross canyon. Though only a few hundred feet away, the two worked in a fluid motion, speaking their own language, the results resting on the forest floor. Robert shook his head in appreciation as he lit a cigarette and crossed his boots, rubbing his knee to ease the stiffness. He was proud of his son, but did not know how to tell him that. He rocked a little as he thought a bit, ignoring Red's tree that landed with a yell, giving way to Billy to proceed. He had rarely given any of his boys a hug and certainly never told any one of them he loved them. It was just not his style. Affection was for the women; the lovers and mothers. Men were men, but he wanted to grab his son and squeeze him, let him know that he meant something to him.

He grunted a bit as he stood up and lifted his binoculars, focusing them on Billy putting in a fast face cut on a rather large alder tree. He cleared his throat, watching as Billy was taking out the tree for a larger fir. Billy began his back cut in a quick, precise fashion. It had a downhill lean and Billy was trying to cut it side hill. His saw set into the rear of the tree and he watched it like he did most trees. But this one surprised him. The trunk split, barber chaired, sending the trunk of the tree at Billy and hitting his side. Billy was pushed back a few feet.

Red and seen it go down from across the shallow canyon and rushed across to see if Billy was all right. Robert quickly leaped from his perch on the hill and fearlessly headed down slope with Hank by his side. The brush was thick and the trees at the upper part of the slope still stood. Red and Billy had started at the

bottom and had worked up hill, and Robert leaped from tree to tree
for support, recklessly slipping and sliding along the steep forest
floor.

He found his son rolling around in the brush, cursing and
yelling, smashing his fist into the ground. Red and Robert stood
silent, breathless, as Hank stopped short of Billy and stood wagging his tail, looking for a stick to chew. Billy was grimacing as he
picked himself up, coughing, wiping the dirt and saw chips off his
clothes.

"Well, you seem to be still breathing," Robert said as he
walked over to a neighboring stump and sat down, lighting a cigarette and throwing a stick for Hank.

"Yeah, I'll be fine. May have broke a rib, that's all," Billy
replied to his father's caring words, leaning to one side and rubbing
his ribs with a hand.

"Think I'm ready for lunch now," the wounded boy said as
he nodded up the hill. Robert picked up Billy's saw and pack, and
led the way out. Red and Hank followed the two up hill toward the
road and down to the truck.

Robert drove the truck back down to the rest of the crew
with Red, Billy and the dog. The crew was laughing and telling
random stories. Many of them had been told and heard already, but
most of the folks could care less. The truck parked and a few
noticed that Billy and Red were in the truck, returning sooner than
expected to the landing. The three men stumbled to the tailgate and
rested against it, eating their sandwiches as the others observed
without much talk.

"You going to be all right?" Robert asked his boy as he
handed him a can of cola.

"It kind of hurts to breathe," Billy replied as he took a large
swig of the cold drink, burping in response, resting his free hand on
the tailgate for support, breathing shallowly, moving little.

"Shit," Robert muttered as he took a large bite out of his
sandwich. The crew watched the father and son talk, and could
make out only a few parts of the conversation. Everyone knew
Billy was hurt, and most were shocked at Robert's somewhat com-
passionate behavior. The wounded boy winced as he ate his sandwich and stared from his feet to the distant canyons and back to his

feet again, ignoring the stares and concerns from others. Normally, Billy would try and give some of the crew shit at lunch, telling jokes and stories, making it a fun time, a much needed break from the work. Today he remained silent and reserved, ignoring everyone as they wrestled around. All folks present were there when Boone had died at Robert's expense, though most blamed Boone for the accident. His dying image remained fresh in their minds, and no hard work or drink could wash it from their thoughts. They only assumed Billy's close call was scare enough for the McDonoughs.

Lunch break was coming to an end when Billy picked himself up and walked toward the choker boys to give them some shit. He smirked at them as he walked, demeaning them with sight and stance. "What happened, dude?" one of them asked as they sat up straight to observe Billy.

"Ah shit, one of them trees barber chaired on me 'n sent me flying. I will make it just fine, just sore," he responded as he reached down to their lunch pail and stole a smoke.

"You lucky sonofabitch," the younger boy said as he put a smoke in his mouth and lit it, exhaling through his nose.

"Yeah, maybe so, 'cept if I died, I would not have to put up with your worthless ass," Billy muttered through the smoke and pain. The crew laughed, as they were waiting for some humor out of the wounded kid. Billy tried not to laugh. Every movement and breath hurt, but he could not help but cough out a few. Billy walked back toward the truck and gave Red and Robert the nod. His father agreed and leaped off the tailgate. Red picked himself up and slapped Billy on the shoulder in an attempt of affection. The three left the crew and returned to the cutting site.

The truck came to the end of the carved out road. All three were staring forward, silently reluctant to finish the day. Robert turned the truck off, placed the keys on the dashboard and rested his hand on the steering wheel. "Well, I guess one of us needs to get something done around here, and it ain't going to be either one of you," Red said as he laughed and left his seat, grabbing his saw and walking off the ridge.

Billy and Robert remained seated, gazing from the truck, looking out the window as the wind pushed the tops of trees in various directions. "I think I'm done for the day, Pops."

Robert nodded in response as he reached for a smoke and looked over at his son. "Yeah, probably don't need to hurt you anymore than you already are." They sat motionless, watching Hank occasionally run in and out of the underbrush, chasing animals and scents. Robert rolled down his window as he lit a smoke, listening to Red scream before he would drop a tree. Billy was content, his mind wandering with the wind, thinking of Annie. His chest and side hurt, but the distractions were enough to pass the time. The two sat silent, bonding as best they knew how, content and worn, weary for the road ahead, accepting the past and the day's work.

21

Annie had parked her mother's truck in the McDonoughs' driveway and brought some much need groceries for the house. The front door was open, and she began putting away dry goods in the cupboards and fresh food in the refrigerator. She had not accomplished much that day, made a little progress on a book that she had been fighting to read, but she wanted to surprise the boys with a home-cooked meal. Her mother never cared much for cooked meals, or the dinner experience of conversations and general appreciations of good food. She often found comfort in TV dinners and scotch. So Annie decided it would be fun and rewarding to make dinner where she knew that it would be appreciated. She also was still weary over what had happened the day before, but wanted to see Billy and continue on with their conversations and smiles.

"Maybe they're at the bar," she said to herself as she poured a glass of water and gazed out the kitchen window toward her mother's truck. It was 4:30 in the afternoon, and she did not know when the crew was generally done with a day, or if they went home first or directly to the bar. She began to wonder if they would be gone for several more hours. Setting down her glass, she smiled as she looked over the pictures and house, and walked to Billy's room, where she leaned against his doorframe and stared at his messy bed. She smiled, then frowned, almost shedding a tear, recalling the recent and the distant past. So much was happening and so much had happened. Where did 10 years go? Where did the careless thoughts and mindless actions hide? Did they ever leave?

Were they back? *What am I doing? What am I thinking?* Annie
stood still, staring with wonder. Within a minute, Billy's truck
came skidding into the driveway. Annie walked into the living
room and watched as Robert and Hank left the truck in a hurry and
headed toward the house. She walked over and opened the door.
Billy took his time, limping.

"I'd give him a little room tonight; he banged himself pretty
good," Robert said as he greeted Annie at his doorway with a smile.
Annie pushed away from the door with concern and walked toward
Billy, who had a cigarette dangling from his lips, a ball cap over his
forehead.

"What happened to you?" Annie asked with a concerned
voice.

"Oh nothing, I just fell down, that's all," he said as he smiled
and rested his arm on her shoulder. They stepped together onto the
deck toward the door as she grabbed his hip with her arm.

"Do you need to see a doctor? It may be a good idea," Annie
spoke softly as she led Billy inside and toward the kitchen. Robert
was standing there, eagerly sipping his first beer. "No babe, I'll be
fine. A few beers, some food, a good night's sleep and I will be
back to normal soon enough," he said as he greeted a beer from his
dad.

"Ever thought of changing professions?" Annie asked in a
humorous way, but causing an uneasy moment of silence. Without
giving it much thought, she corrected herself. "Well, it's your lucky
day, boys. I went shopping and am going to cook you two a grand
meal." She grabbed a pot and began cooking. Billy watched his
father respond to her comment and excuse himself to his room.

"You look pretty today," Billy said, looking Annie over. Her
skirt exposed her clean, tan legs, her blouse half unbuttoned. Billy
propped himself up against the kitchen counter, gazing outside at
the weather. Annie smiled in response.

"Is it all right that I'm here?"

"Of course. It's nice having you around…'n I am sore, so it
works out great. I may need some special attention tonight," he
said, smiling as he reached for his second beer, passing one to
Annie, who shook her head at his comment.

"Why don't you get out of the kitchen and go take a shower," she said, walking toward Billy and leaning up to give him a kiss.

"Yeah, I probably should," he said, nodding in agreement and carrying his beer toward the bathroom to get clean. Surprisingly, she was enjoying herself more than she thought she would. Annie had never been too domesticated, but the thought of bringing some comfort into Billy's life was, in many ways, means for forgiveness from their past and recent losses. She had often searched for the love she'd lost a decade ago with Billy, and there was a subtle comfort and peace of mind that had never re-entered her life. She'd found herself smiling randomly the last couple days.

"You going to be around awhile?" Robert asked, interrupting her thoughts as he walked into the kitchen for another beer. Annie paused, simply nodding and shrugging her shoulders. Robert knew his son well enough to know that he was starting to fall for this woman again. Annie raised her eyes from the pasta and placed them on Robert.

"I don't know, but the trip back here has been very peaceful so far, and I like that."

Robert had seen other women come and go with Billy, mostly in rapid fashion. He knew that love could send either of them down avenues that they were not ready to discover or accept. She was an educated woman in an uneducated town, and he was curious and willing to seek and do other things. The old man enjoyed the presence of women, but was generally skeptical with Billy and the effect it had on work. Robert always assumed the worst, and he figured his boy would some day run off. He peered at Annie and glanced at the food with a smile. "Well, it's good to have you here."

Silence sat between them as she stirred the pasta sauce and placed the spaghetti into the boiling water. They could hear some faint Hank Williams lyrics from the shower where Billy gracefully sang. Annie began to chuckle at his performance and Robert shook his head.

"You know, he always does that, and he is a horrible singer," Robert said with a laugh.

22

The week rolled on by rather quickly as Billy took it easy and nursed his wounds. Billy and Robert left Red in charge and traveled around the area evaluating future projects and locations. The two worked short days. This was not uncommon, but generally Robert did this on his own. Billy was more useful in the field, but even Robert in his stubbornness realized his kid needed a break from time to time.

For a few nights that week, Annie stayed over and helped around the house. She was a bit bored during the day, but kept herself busy reading and picking up at her mother's house and at Billy's. She had always had a difficult time sleeping through the night in the cities, for no certain reason why. But, the last several weeks she was able to sleep long hours and refresh herself. Without the worries of work, or the hustle and bustle of the city and friends, cocktails and gyms, she was able to pace herself at a gentle stride.

Their nights were spent in each other's arms, arguing about old friends and stories, listening to records and sipping beers. Robert was around from time to time, but would often leave them be, heading to Ray's Place or into his room. Robert was content. It had been a nice change to work with Billy every day, just the two of them driving around and scouting sites, meeting with folks about projects and taking a step back from the crew. Red was getting the work done. The crew was hitting 20 loads a day and pulling it off with just a little bit of overtime.

By Friday, Robert had most of his jobs planned out for several months. Lee was on board with cutting out needed roads and the paperwork was in order. They took their time getting ready that morning. Annie helped Billy cook a large breakfast before she kicked the men out to work. Robert wanted to take a look at their piece of land in Cadillac. It had been awhile since they had done that. They drove up the ridges and hills, the windy road weaving its way around until they entered the little mill town. They stopped at a high point in town and stared at the plywood mill. The lake was high from the spring rains; the sounds of machines and engines spoke softy in the distance. The hillsides had come back with replanted trees, much of it young in age, different generations of re-growth.

Their stringer of land ran right along town, separating the mill at points from the mill housing that was nearby. Their tall trees looked like a Mohawk running down slope until it settled on the valley floor. "Don't think I will ever cut this piece just to piss them off," Robert said as he lit a cigarette and leaned back in the truck seat.

Billy nodded. "Looks funny sitting there though. Everything else cut 'n our little piece hanging on."

Robert looked at Billy. "That piece of land has been in our family since the turn of the century," he said. Robert paused and took a drag of his smoke. "That land has survived three different mill owners since they first moved in years ago. I know we can get top dollar for that wood, but I don't really give a damn about that."

Billy nodded. He knew the story, but Robert felt the need to enlighten him again. "At one point, the first logging company owned 85,000 acres. Now I think Columbia is down to 60,000 and even at that, maybe only a few thousand is left to log. Everything else is still too small; will be for years to come. That mill ain't gonna last much longer; it just can't."

Billy rolled down his window and spit outside, then wrestled a little with his ball cap before it rested comfortably on his head. "Guess we'll have to drive our logs a bit further then."

Robert looked at Billy with a frown. "Yeah, but if Creekville's mill closes too, then it's a certain jump to the next mill." Columbia would stay afloat a bit on the McDonough land if they were to sell it off, not just the stringer in town, but they owned several hundred acres on the outskirts of Columbia's land. Most of it was second growth, close to harvest, but Robert generally took other folks' contracts on their owned land. His crew had logged thousands of Columbia's acres in the past.

"Never thought I'd see the day when it would come to an end, but it's knocking at the door. You will see, son…one day everything is up and running, men are working, next day everything will shut down. There just ain't no more certainty in this work, not sure there ever was." Robert returned his attention to the distant mill. "Hell, people still wipe their asses and we still send our logs across the ocean to the Orient, but ain't no damn politician wants to get in the way of the larger boys, or some owl or fish. I don't know, just did not think I would see the day, not with all the land out here, not with all the trees."

Billy took his hat off and placed it on the dashboard. "Well, it ain't happened yet, Pops."

Robert chuckled. "Yeah, well it's here, we just don't know it quite yet." Robert started the truck and headed down the hill into the town. Billy grabbed his hat and put it back on. The two sat silent and watched the town as they drove slowly through it in search of the café for a quick meal. They were not considered locals, but certainly not strangers. They rarely came to Cadillac; just did not have much of a need, even though their log trucks often did. It was tucked away in the hills. The road systems were pretty rough and often washed out. The few hundred residents rarely left. The mill provided nearly all the work and most of the buildings were owned and maintained by the company, even the café. The school district remained separate and there was a lot of talk regarding the new gym that was recently built. No one wanted to see that torn down. It was a sign of the possibility of the future, a reason to smile, distracting their concerns and pushing back the rumors.

The two entered the small establishment and smiled as they recognized a few familiar faces. They were kindly greeted with coffee and menus. Neither bothered to look at them, knowing that burgers would do the trick that day. They ate without much conversation. Friendly nods and handshakes interrupted their lunch, but the food tasted good and allowed both to think their thoughts. One of the foremen for some of the equipment in town walked up to Robert and slapped him on the shoulder, somewhat rough, but friendly. "You going to sell your chunk of land over there?"

Robert finished his last bite and wiped his mouth with his napkin, quickly glancing at Billy before responding, "Got no intentions of it, Sammy."

The other man stood shaking his head. "There ain't much more here to log unless the company starts buying out other folks' land."

Robert nodded and looked Sammy in the eyes. "Yeah, it seems that way, don't it? But, I don't think our little pieces are going to help much unless they bid on that stuff just west of here with Mackenzie Logging."

Sammy stood, looking out the window at the mill. "Yeah, been a few rumors about that. Doesn't sound like talks are that good for that happening. I guess Columbia just got some new board members and such back in Atlanta. Not sure if they will cut us all loose or not. Who knows? Been here in town for 30 years and it seems like every few years they talk about closing us down, but we still plug away." Robert smiled and understood. Both had been around long enough to see their assumptions come true and some come up false. But, they just were not producing nearly the board feet they did even five years prior, and eventually someone would have to cut it off.

Robert stood up, grabbed the check, and looked Sammy in the eye. "Good to see you again, old man." The two smiled and exchanged handshakes as Sammy put on his ball cap and walked out the door. Billy sat still in his seat, playing with a toothpick in his mouth, watching as Sammy walked toward the mill. Robert came back to the table, placed a bill on it for a tip, and headed for the door. Billy got up, grimacing a little in response to his ribs, which felt better, but sometimes caught him off guard.

They drove through town and up toward the winding road back to Hemlock. Both knew it was time for a cold one and to hear what stories and lies Ray had to say.

The afternoon was still young when Red and the crew piled in for their Friday beers. Robert was finishing signing their checks and began handing them out. Some left once they got their check, others stayed for awhile. "Got to get it while you can; summer shut downs will be soon," Robert said as he handed the checks to the choker boys, knowing that their longer shifts could give way to shorter ones, earlier work, and quick pushes through the days.

Minutes passed by slowly as the remaining crew massaged the ideas with drinks. The bar was still pretty empty, a quiet time before the after-work Friday night push. The two McDonoughs sat alone, initially in silence, Billy often staring at the door. Robert noticed and smiled. "You like that girl, don't you?"

Billy returned his attention to his dad. "Yeah, I always did, even when she left for so long. Not sure what it is, just feels good, you know?"

"Not sure if it's true or not, but someone told me something one time to the effect of you can't be wise and in love at the same time, just can't happen," Robert said, taking a drag and looking over his boy. "Not sure if that saying is worth a shit. I knew the second I laid eyes on your mother many years ago that she was the one. I was done running around and as much as I fought it, I couldn't." Billy nodded as he looked his father over, his wrinkles exposed on his forehead. Robert continued, "I never thought I would live without her, figured I would go first…I can't believe she put up with me for so long. I know I ain't easy, but it's the only way I know." Robert bit his lips, massaging his hands as he laid the burning cigarette in the ashtray, eyes squinted, focusing on the mirror and bottles in front of him.

Billy remained silent. No one bothered the two as they talked about mom. Everyone knew there was some rather important conversation going on. Ray even kept his distance, even though both their drinks were empty. Billy broke the silence. "She loved you, Dad, not because of longevity, but because you were true, an honest man, for better or worse." Billy squeezed the lump in his throat, doing his best to hold back any tears.

Robert nodded, taking a drag, looking over at Billy quickly before staring back at the mirror. "She really loved all you boys, and I know she hated the fact you and Boone took up logging. She hated it and never once complained to me about it." A brief moment of silence passed and the back door slammed as someone exited the bathroom.

"Yeah, she loved all of us, Pops." Billy said as he watched his father's trigger hand tremble.

"She was always right. Not sure how or why, but she was always right," Robert said as he reached for his glass, realizing as he lifted it that it was empty.

Both their eyes sat damp. They were unwilling to shed any tears, unwilling to rest a hand on each other. Robert lit another smoke, accepting the silence and conversation, though it was difficult for him. He paused, hesitated, before asking, "Do you ever wish you took off outta here like Junior?"

"And leave you behind?" Billy asked smiling.

"I'm serious, damn it!" Robert returned with a stern voice, causing Billy to lose his smile.

"No, I don't think about that much. I have in the past, but don't know what I'd do or where I'd go." Billy talked as he stared at his empty glass. He could feel his father's eyes resting upon him.

"Well, I have been second guessing things lately," Robert whispered as he took a drag of his smoke. This caught Billy off guard. He had his concerns, especially since Boone and Mom's deaths, but there was never anything said or really shown.

"Like what?" Billy whispered back in response. No one needed to hear this.

"Like losing you, logging, all this shit, I just don't know anymore," Robert said, shaking his head and looking at Billy. "Ever since the accident and your mom's passing, 'n then for Christ sakes, you the other day getting hit. Man, it's a sign. God is a telling me something."

"I ain't going to leave you, Pops," Billy said as he rested his arm on his father's shoulder and dragged him close. Robert did not fight the show of affection. He just went limp and rocked. They sat silent, staring at their empty glasses, both pondering, lost in unknowns.

The door opened and Lee walked in. "Hey, you sonofabitch," Robert yelled at Lee as he separated from Billy's grip, nodding at Ray for a round.

"Shit, Bob, you talk to me nicer than my old lady does," Lee said, smiling and giving the nod to Ray for a drink.

Robert took one last glance at Billy, his eyes telling his boy his story, quickly turning to Lee. "Yeah, 'n I'm prettier then she is, too." Everyone in the bar that heard Robert's response was laughing. Lee chuckled as he took his first sip of the day, taking a deep breath and unable to send another dig toward Robert. Instead, he sat down by his old friend as they tore into working stories.

Billy stared into the bar mirror, evaluating his look. He parted his hair with his hand and cracked his neck. He pretended not to listen to his father and Lee's conversation about some upcoming work. Minutes later, the door gently opened and a clean-cut young man entered the room, hesitant but intent. He was well dressed and it was obvious that he was not from around there. Everyone watched the stranger take a seat a few seats from Billy.

Ray walked slowly toward the young man. "What can I get you, son?"

"Hello there. Can I have a Bombay martini up and dry?"

Billy smirked as he heard the request for the drink.

"Sorry son, no can do," Ray said, throwing his bar towel over his shoulder.

"Okay, how about a Jameson on the rocks?"

"That I can do, son," Ray replied with a grin as he reached for a whiskey glass and dipped into a tub of ice before filling it with the Irish drink. No one continued on with their conversations for a minute or two. It was not that unusual, especially on a Friday, to see some strangers come in, but this kid was just a little more far removed than most.

"Where are you from, stranger?" Billy asked the guy as he took a sip from his whiskey, coughing in response.

"Seattle."

Billy lifted his back. "What brings you to Hemlock? It's a bit out of the way." He spoke both at the stranger and in Ray's direction, signaling for another beer. Ray handed a full glass of draft, whispering, "Here you go, Billy."

The stranger lifted his head at the exchange. The man replied, "I'm looking for someone."

Robert and Lee stopped talking as they both searched for one of their cigarettes. They watched in curiosity at the younger boys' conversation.

"Who are you looking for?" Billy asked, sipping his beer.

"Annie Sutton."

"Oh yeah?"

"I assume you are Billy McDonough," the stranger said as he stared briefly into Billy's curious but aggressive eyes.

Billy nodded, "Yes, I am."

"Well then, excuse me," the stranger said as he picked himself up and walked away to a corner table.

"Do I smell?" Billy turned in his bar stool as he watched the man walk away. The man ignored Billy's question as he sat down and lit a smoke. Billy rose from his stool and walked toward him. "I asked you if I smell?" Billy repeated himself. He was not used to folks turning their backs on him, let alone having to repeat himself. He set down his beer at the man's table and placed both hands on a nearby chair, resting himself upright.

"Look, I am not going to fight you or argue with you, I am just here to see Annie. I know she came back here, and I assume you have seen her. I have heard some stories and I need to talk with her, okay?" Billy nodded as he patiently listened to the man's explanation. The man continued, "I am not sure why she is here; not sure why anyone lives here."

Billy smiled as he wiped his mouth free of the excess beer. Robert and Lee had been listening and watching, and Robert picked himself up from the bar stool and threw down his smoke on the bar floor, crushed it out with his boot, exhaling toward the seated stranger.

"What the fuck you say, faggot?" Robert asked in an aggressive voice. The stranger was beginning to get a little uneasy in his seat, staring up at the larger Billy and an older angry guy moving in fast. The man sat silent, trying to keep his mouth shut. He was not used to that, but in this circumstance, it may have been his best approach. "Listen to me, you little city boy queer, this here is my boy. Don't you go disrespecting him, especially not here in front of me or my friends," Robert said as he lifted his boot and placed it on the neighboring seat, leaning in, waiting for a response. By this time, everyone in the bar was facing the stranger, waiting eagerly to see his response.

Billy caught the stranger's eyes as the two read into them. "Look, I am sure you are a nice guy, or at least an intelligent one, so it would be smart of you to pick yourself up and walk out of here before you get carried out." The stranger paused and finished his drink in a sip, got up and quickly scanned down the bar. He grabbed his sunglasses and walked out, muttering, "Fucking hillbillies."

"What the fuck you say, motherfucker?" Robert yelled as he charged for the door, Billy caught his dad and needed the assistance of Lee to contain him. The man skirted out as quickly as he could. Robert's face was fire engine red as he kicked and yelled drunken cries at the young man. The door opened as the young man was about to leave and Annie appeared, stopping in her tracks in surprise.

"What are you doing here?" she asked, confused and slowly realizing the developing situation.

She grabbed his arm and led him outside as he mumbled, "I wanted to talk with you. You just packed up and left, and I couldn't really understand your letter...what did you expect me to do?" By now they were outside, walking in the middle of the parking lot.

Billy let go of his dad, who was still agitated. "Can you believe the nerve of that little fuck?" Robert walked back to his drink and nodded for bourbon. Ray returned, lining the three men up with shots. Robert shot his back before the other two even touched their glasses. None of them could make out the argument outside. Billy watched Annie as she spoke, making out some of the conversation through the open window.

"I don't want you anymore. I don't know what I want," she said as she wiped the hair from her eyes and folded her arms.

"I will change," the ex-fiancé pleaded.

"Too late."

"So, what is it? Billy walks back into your life and flips your world upside down?"

"Listen, it's different."

"Do you love him?"

"I don't know."

"Do you still love me?"

"I don't know!" She released her arms and placed them on her hips, again trying desperately to get her hair from blowing in her eyes. He stood silent, leaning against his Mercedes. "I just know right now I feel better than I have in awhile."

"What about your job and the firm?" he said as he tried to make eye contact. She avoided it as much as possible.

"I am still on leave, said it was a family thing, and I told them I would get back to them."

"Why?" he demanded.

"I don't have an answer for you, because I don't have an answer for myself."

"I thought you loved our life, the city, the travels…"

"I did, I do, but being with you made me want to change."

The man fell back harder against his car, surprised by her comment. He had bought her whatever she wanted, taken her to many great places near and far, and waited on her hand and foot. They sat speechless and watched as a few townsfolk looked at the foreign car and the two standing in the gravel parking lot. Annie hated the fact that he had shown up there. He never once wanted to drive down and visit her hometown. She never really did either, but it still frustrated her. She knew he loved her, but nothing he could do or say right now would make her get in that car and leave with him.

"Well, I really enjoyed myself when I was with you," he said as he opened up his car door and sat down, starting the ignition and finding a gear.

Annie grinned and knelt down to look at his eyes. "In many ways I still love you, but I need to do this." He smiled back and drove off, heading eastbound out of town. She watched as his tail-lights disappeared into the early evening shadows.

Annie walked slowly toward the bar, feeling a little embarrassed and angry. She was uncertain about her life in so many ways. Things were comfortable right now, and seeing her ex made all her lingering uncertainties vividly real. She pushed the door open and could feel the place get silent. Billy had heard much of their conversation, and continued to smoke his cigarette and glance at her. She raised her head just to find a seat near Billy. Ray walked over with a smile and set down a cold draft for her. She nodded, then asked for a shot of vodka.

Ray returned with a chilled glass and the drink. She shot it back, sending her hair whipping around, some of it landing on Billy's shoulder. He shook his head in disbelief. Robert was still upset, but held back from any comments. He nodded at Lee for a game of pool. They left the two sitting there.

It did not take long before Annie began crying. Billy let her drown momentarily in her tears before acknowledging it by placing his large arm around her back and scooting her close. She welcomed the gesture and rested her head against his chest. Her tears started to make his shirt wet, and she laughed and blew her nose on a napkin. She cleared her throat. "You stink."

Billy took a long sip from his beer and responded, "Do I? I thought I did?"

"What?" She did not understand his response.

"Don't worry about it."

She lifted her face, her eyes red and a little swollen from tears. "I'm sorry, Billy."

"Yeah, that's all right."

"Do you want to get out of here?" she said as she took a sip from her beer.

Billy nodded. He waved at his father and Ray, and they shouted obscenities back at him as he finished her beer in a few swigs.

They left as the sun was beginning to set over the ridge. Billy walked straight toward his door and opened it, then started the truck as he watched Annie get in. She looked at him for a second and smiled before putting her seat belt on. He watched her. "Do you want me to take you to your mom's house or are you coming over?"

She cleared her throat and talked in a quiet voice. "I want to be with you tonight." Billy nodded, threw the truck in a quick reverse and skidded out of the parking lot. He was frustrated with her and other things. The past couple of weeks had been fun and exciting, but he finally had taken a step back to realize what was going on. He shook his head as he went around a sharp curve.

"I heard some of your conversation."

Annie took her head away from the window and placed her eyes on him. "I had to say what I had to say to get him out of here. I don't want him here. I don't know what I want."

Billy listened, biting his lip. He knew that sometimes his words, like his father's, got him into trouble, but he spoke up anyway. "Well, what the fuck am I supposed to think?" Annie shook her head without a response. "Are you just a piece of ass or what?"

Annie glared at Billy, who appeared upset, sending the truck hard into a few turns as he rubbed his tongue against his lower teeth.

"I hope that is not what you think of me," Annie said as she folded her arms and looked at Billy. He shrugged his shoulders and stepped on the gas.

The silence was thick and wearisome for both of them. She broke it by shaking her head and muttering, "Listen, things are really confusing for me right now, Billy…I like you, I enjoy you, and that is all I can really say about us right now."

Billy nodded. "I just think if you are going to pick up and go again, you should do it now before it gets harder, that's all."

Annie nodded and thought for a second. "I don't want to go anywhere right now."

"I don't want to love you again," Billy said as he wove in between a few large, overhanging trees and slowed into their driveway.

Annie shook her head with an understanding that they shared. "I know what you mean, but something is making it hard to go, and I don't want to run from it right now."

Billy cleared his throat as he tossed the keys on the dashboard and opened his door. Annie sat motionless for a moment before she left the truck for the house. Billy stood in the living room looking around as she walked in. She moved slowly towards him and rested her arms around his neck, "I don't want to go anywhere. I think I am falling for you again and I have never felt this way before. I am just scared." Billy rested his hands around her lower back and grimaced at the slight pressure on his ribs. She smiled and moved a little to help him out. He said nothing as their lips touched for a moment.

"Let's go to bed," Annie said as she separated herself from his soft grip. She walked over to his room and began getting undressed until she was naked, slowly getting into the cold bed. He watched her from the doorway as he knelt to untie his boots. She watched him as he took his time taking off his clothes.

"I should probably shower, but I don't think I will," he said with a smile. Annie grinned back, shaking her head in disgust.

They nestled close together and in a matter of minutes, Annie was fast asleep and quietly breathing against Billy's chest. He lay there listening to her breathe as his mind backtracked through the day. It was a long day and his weary body and mind felt its fatigue. His father's concerns about life and work, and Annie's run-in with her ex, left Billy confused at so many levels, but the tiredness overtook his worries as he fell into a deep sleep.

A few hours later he was awakened by a dream. He sat there breathing hard, dreaming of Boone. They had been throwing a football around the yard as they did when they were younger. Billy wiped some sweat off his forehead and softly separated himself from Annie. He walked into the kitchen and fixed himself a sandwich. He sat alone in the living room eating, listening to the howling wind beat against the house. Annie had rolled over, gotten up from the bed, grabbed one of Billy' shirts and put it on, then opened the door to find Billy eating in the dim living room light. He smiled at her as he gobbled down the large sandwich. She walked over and he handed over the remains of the sandwich. She accepted the remaining few bits and with a mouthful of food, she spoke. "Good dinner." They both laughed. They lifted each other up and returned back to the warm bed.

23

The morning came and went like so many that followed, and cool, breezy spring afternoons turned quickly into the hotter days of summer. The crew continued to produce throughout this time, gearing up for summer shutdowns and occasionally felling assignments of wildfires around the state. McDonough's equipment was still in fair shape and for the most part, besides a few bruises here and there, the crew was working well, producing, staying healthy, and meshing well as a unit.

Many of the nights found Billy and Annie together, and when Billy was not working long days, they would often disappear to the falls for a quick swim and lay. On repeated occasions, Annie tried to get closer to her mother, but her efforts were lost in her mother's smoke and scotch. Annie had all but moved into Billy and Robert's house. Most of her time was spent volunteering at the small public library or at the school with her friend Susie. She had put in a few interest letters to small law firms in the valley just to see if something might open up. She missed practicing law, though she had done it for only a few years.

Annie was succeeding in some ways. On the weekends, she would convince Billy to drive to the valley to watch a movie and go out to dinner. Billy enjoyed the trips, as he enjoyed most of the things he did with Annie. Their curious interest in one another did not slip or stagnate, but in many ways grew. She often wore tight shorts or wavy skirts in the early summer sun, giving Billy easier access when desired or just a pleasant sight for his eyes.

The early stages of summer brought warmer, drier conditions to the residents of Hemlock as it headed to July fourth. The celebration was always entertaining at Ray's Place, where people brought their home-cooked meals and barbecued on the back deck all day long. If you brought food and were a local, then all the draft beer was free. The back deck was the most crowded place to be, with many of the old-timers hanging inside in the darkness, while the rowdy crowd yelled and screamed on the deck. Often arguments and near fights would break out over who was in charge of the barbecue.

Annie and Billy spent much of the afternoon on the deck, sipping beers and lying in each other's arms, casting long stares at each other when they would get up for a refill or indulge in a brief conversation with someone else.

Billy walked toward Annie, who was laughing and talking with Susie. "Come here for a second, babe." Annie nodded and excused herself, taking Billy's hand as they walked from the bar toward his truck. He opened the door, picked her up and laid her down, quickly scanning the parking lot before he looked back at her. She forcefully grabbed his neck and pushed her tongue against his. He raised his hand and grazed her breasts, sending her nipples to harden. He lifted himself up long enough to unzip and pull down his pants and underwear. She wrestled with hers, and he helped slide them down her legs, her summer dress still on though lifted above her stomach. He pushed in as she gasped, and the truck began to slightly rock as they moved back in forth. The cab was hot, the sun beating down from the afternoon heat. They were quickly covered with sweat as they continued on before coming to a resting halt. Breathing hard, they laughed, not wanting to separate or move. She leaned up and bit his chin as he jerked away in surprise. Then he watched her grind her teeth and blink her eyes uncontrollably. She shook a bit and pulled him close as she breathed hard and shook. She let out a gasp with a smile and opened her eyes. He was entertained watching her. She smiled and placed a soft, wet kiss on his lips. He picked himself up and watched her lying there, sweat beginning to fall from his head and chest onto her legs.

"You hungry?" Billy asked as he chuckled, zipping up his pants and searching for a cigarette.

"Yes, I am," Annie said as she put her underwear back on beneath her dress.

"Think they missed us?"

"Not likely," she said smiling, grabbing him again and sending him back down on her, forcing his lips against hers.

He pushed himself off. "Jesus, what the fuck got into you?" Annie lifted herself up and looked in the mirror to fix her hair, licked her lips and smiled at him. He opened the door and grabbed an old shirt to wipe off his sweat. He felt a bit dizzy as he leaned against his truck. The summer heat, the beer and sex sent him in various directions. He peered toward the bar to watch his dad stumble outside with a beer in his hand. Robert struggled as he began pissing on Tommy's car, the one that actually ran. Annie and Billy laughed as they watched him carve urine letters over his hood and tire. Annie leaned over and kissed Billy.

"I'm going to go find some food. Don't you run off now," she said.

Billy smiled back at Annie before turning his attention to his father. "How are you holding up, Pops?" Robert stumbled at the question. One hand held his beer, the other tried to zip up the flood gates.

"Oh, just a little drunk, n' angry with the damn contracts and other companies." Robert wiped his mouth, slurring his speech.

"Oh shit, relax," Billy said as he helped his dad slowly walk toward the front door. He knew his dad was under a lot of stress. Three mills across the state had closed in the last two months. There were talks of closing the mill in Creekville, too. If this happened, along with Cadillac shutting down, then their logging turnarounds could be far, and their commuting time between work sites difficult.

Robert began to balance his thoughts. "If the mill goes down, Billy, we are going to be hurting. It ain't what we got now, it's what we got four months from now. Our equipment is old and needs to be replaced." His words slurred as he rambled along.

"How do you know Columbia is going under?"

"Ah hell, the company is making profits, but Cadillac is losing money and board feet. It's just a numbers game to them fuckers." Robert leaned against a truck and lit a cigarette.

Billy convinced his dad that it was not the time to talk about work, not today, not after a good lay and a good drink. "Listen, Pops, let's go drink 'till we are full."

The two men walked slowly to the back deck where they were greeted by Lee shouting, "And here is to the McDonough sons of bitches!" Everyone cheered and displayed their appreciation, lighting fireworks in various directions. One started a small grass fire, where Lee found himself kicking dirt and spilling beer on it until the volunteers showed up to put it out. Annie welcomed Billy with a fresh cheeseburger and a kiss. He gladly wolfed down the food. The night brought a cool breeze as they finished the keg and tapped another. By midnight, Billy was stumbling around, hanging onto Annie's shoulder, talking about high school football with an old teammate. Robert was passed out in a lawn chair on the deck with Lee by his side in another. Annie was far more sober, and guided Billy toward the truck and drove them home.

24

Billy awoke to Annie wrestling around in the bed. He did not think much of it as he barely lifted an eye. Robert was outside cursing at an old saw that he had been meaning to fix for some time now. Annie lay still again, listening to Robert curse the saw and the dog. She reached over, grabbed Billy's cock and rubbed it. Billy lay still in surprise. Annie listened as his father cursed randomly in a hung-over fashion and eventually opened the back door. His boot steps were getting closer and the smell of cigarettes began to enter closer to their room.

Robert knocked once and heard no reply so he entered. Annie picked her head from the pillow and smiled at the old man. He shouted at Billy, who was motionless, "I got a meeting with Columbia Logging today, so you got the crew."

Billy wiped his face with his hand and tried to concentrate. "I thought we were off today," the younger boy spoke in a still drunken morning voice.

"Yeah, I changed my mind. Put in a half day, and that should be enough to get all the logs off of the Eagle Rim project. I told Red that it would be a bit before you got there." Robert smiled at the two lying in bed, knowing that Billy was not in any shape to work.

Billy nodded. "Yeah, it's going to be a bit before I get out of bed."

Robert shook his head in approval. "Just try and get that equipment moved to the next site near Smith Creek today."

The old man left the younger crowd to wake up as he walked outside, started his truck and took off for a meeting. Annie slipped her hand back down over Billy, who laid his head back down on his pillow and smiled. Annie began kissing her way down to his cock before rubbing her lips over him until he was finished. Billy was beginning to feel better; his pain subsided with distraction; his mind still heavy but content.

"I guess we're not heading out today?" Annie asked as she got up and searched for a glass of water.

"Guess not," Billy said as he walked naked toward the bathroom. He returned to find Annie dressed and eager to do something. "This should not take long. Pops is just eager to get as much done as he can, paranoid at the possible mill closings."

Annie smiled and watched Billy get dressed, then let a sigh that was louder than intended. "Are you going to be able to take a few days off?"

Billy looked up at her, walked to the bed and sat down. "I think I could. You thinking you want to go camping or something?"

"I just want a few days to myself with you," she said, sad that he always was involved with work.

"Well, with this weather, I just don't see us putting in a whole day for awhile now."

Annie tried not to smile, but she could not help it. She wanted to visit the farmers' markets in nearby towns, walk the coastline just over the mountains, hit the road and see where it took them. Billy had expressed interest in many of these adventures, but every day, every week, seemed to bring some sort of work stress or requirement.

Annie slapped her hand on Billy's leg as she bounced out of bed and headed for the kitchen. "C'mon, I'll make you an egg."

Billy squinted as he bent over to tie his boots, his head heavy, feeling each heartbeat like it was a sledgehammer beating against his melon. "This is going to be interesting," he muttered as he searched for some aspirin.

He could hear the eggs frying in the kitchen as Annie sang to herself. Billy paused and listened, and enjoyed her voice, soft and sweet. He could not make out the song, but it echoed gently against the rising morning sun. It was already warm, and his throat was raw from too many drinks and cigarettes. His eyes ached from the sun and his search for sunglasses was unsuccessful.

She found Billy resting his head against the table, then handed him the plate with two eggs and a few pieces of toast. The thought was nice and Billy smiled, but the reality of eating was not something he was too fond of. He ate slowly, pondering how the food would sit in his stomach, taking only a few sips from his cup of coffee. Annie watched as she enjoyed her eggs, taking her time to chew and swallow. Billy looked at her, face flushed, eyes sagging, and hair in a mess.

"You look like shit," she said as she chewed some toast.

Billy shook his head in utter disgust. "Feel like it, too. Well, let me go do this shit and get on with it."

Annie watched as he went out the door and started his truck. He sat momentarily in the cab, as if to let the engine warm up on a winter's morning. Annie finished her plate, grabbed his and brought it to the sink. She looked out the window and saw Billy resting his head against the steering wheel. She chuckled and began walking toward the door, but he finally came to grips with reality and slowly drove off. She stood on the deck and let the morning breeze lift her shirt slightly and blow her hair.

Billy arrived at Red's house to find him outside, napping in his chair. Red slowly walked to the truck and threw his gear in the back. "Well, I feel like shit. What the fuck was your dad thinking?" Billy just shook his head and rested on his left hand for support as they turned around and left Red's place.

Not many words were spoken between the two as they arrived at the landing to greet the rest of the wounded crew. Billy parked the truck and got out. He walked toward the center of the men, who moved in a little closer to hear their briefing. "All right, listen up. For some reason, Pops wants this shit picked up today and moved to the other site on the other ridge." He paused and coughed. "Shouldn't take all that long to do. This ain't my decision. I'm thinking my dad is losing it. He has been meeting with some of the companies and he fears that they are going to shut down Cadillac and even Creekville…nothing is for sure; nothing has been said."

"What do you think?" one of the choker boys asked as he took a dip.

"There ain't much for Columbia to cut at Cadillac, even if we did sell them our little pieces, and besides Smith, we are the only ones bringing wood to them. I just don't see them staying open," Billy said as he stared at the curious kid. "But listen, we got some work now, whether we want it or not. Pops has several projects lined out."

Someone mentioned the mill in Creekville and Billy jerked his head in response. "Don't know about that much, but if that closes, we are fucked. Turnaround times are going to be a bitch and you might have to move if you want to log."

"Bullshit," shouted Larry, the loader operator for the day. "I'm third generation logger here. I can see for miles and miles of timber waiting to get cut."

Billy lit a smoke and nodded in agreement. "Trust me, Larry, I know what you mean. Hell, I'm fourth generation. You know that. We just don't own enough land or new equipment to run and gun with the big boys, and you know they just are not going to cut the public shit like they use to."

"Well, who the fuck can we talk to then?" Larry shouted as he reached for his dip.

"Those cocksuckers don't live around here, Larry, they live in high-rise apartments and big homes elsewhere. I bet the board members have not even been to Cadillac and seen the way of life or how the folks depend on that mill and town." Everyone began to nod; many were frustrated and hung over.

"Listen, I am trying to be optimistic. I've known many of you since I was just a kid, know your families and your thoughts without you even speaking, but the times ahead could be different than we are used to." As Billy spoke, the sun beat against his back and felt good. The aspirin had taken its effect and his head not as heavy as before.

"All right guys, let's get these loads off the hill and move the equipment down the road," Billy said as he returned to his truck and nodded at Red, who shook his head in agreement.

25

Robert headed for a restaurant in Dallas to meet with some of the corporate heads of Columbia Logging. He arrived at the same time as his old partner, Gary Smith, did. The two of them were responsible for most of the logging that went on in the county. Both had worked and lived there their whole lives. They greeted each other with handshakes and smiles. They were competitive and both ran good, honest crews. Smith was more of a reserved, more professional owner than Robert was. Robert called it like he saw it and would not hesitate to break someone down if he felt it needed to be done.

Smith shook his head as he grabbed Robert's hand for a firm shake. "Not sure this is going to be good, Robert."

"Well, at his point I don't know what to think anymore, Gary. These sons of bitches come in and are probably going to close down the mills. They buy out each other like they're doing their Sunday laundry. People are griping about birds and owls, and sending our wood across the ocean, and I just don't know. A lot has changed since we started."

They stood there, Gary spitting out the rest of his dip. "Robert, I told my boys to move on out of this neck of the woods if they want to raise a family."

Robert shook his head. "I know, but I ain't ready to give up just yet."

Gary turned and followed Robert into the restaurant where they looked in the back and saw a few well-dressed gentlemen seated at a table, sipping coffee and observing the two older woodsmen walk toward them.

One of the younger men stood up and greeted them. "Which one of you is Gary and which one of you is Robert?"

The two looked at each other as if to lie for the hell of it, but both chose not to. Gary spoke and introduced himself; Robert did the same as he lit a cigarette.

"We don't normally do this to folks - that is, take the time to come out to the sites and introduce ourselves. Most of our time is spent locked up in the office arguing about numbers and board feet, and so on and so forth."

"Sounds tiring," Robert said, smiling at the man, their eyes connecting long enough for the younger one to glance away. He turned back. "We are here to tell you that we will no longer give out any more contracts on our land and we no longer need your services."

Gary leaned back in his chair. "Listen, I know me and Robert bring you guys a lot of wood, buying you plenty of these here lunches and sport jackets."

"That don't make no goddamn sense!" Robert griped as he nodded in approval to the waitress for some coffee.

"Listen, we know that you two have some land around Cadillac, but it does not matter. That old mill is falling apart and it is not making us any money anymore. Now, I can't speak for the other mill just up the road, but we are going to be closing our doors soon."

The other businessman began to open his mouth, but Robert interrupted. "I got men who have worked for me for 20 years, got men who are second, third, even fourth generation loggers out there spilling blood and sweat for me, doing whatever I ask them to do. What the fuck am I going to tell them? What the fuck are they going to tell their kids?"

"We are not in the business of family counseling, sir," the oldest of the three said as he lit a cigarette.

"Don't you call me sir, you little faggot. I work for a living!" Robert snarled at him, clenching his fist.

"Listen, we don't normally do this. We will go public soon enough. It may be as long as six to nine months before we close the town down - I mean, the mill."

Both Robert and Gary looked at one another and then looked back. Gary spoke first. "Close the town down?"

"No, he meant the mill," the older gentleman said as he leaned back and stared at Robert.

Robert shook his head. "Why'd you call us in here?"

"We want to buy your land for a fair price in the town and a bit around it, Robert. According to our records, you own more land than Gary does in that area."

Robert looked at Gary and shook his head. "Yeah, and it ain't for sale, neither."

Gary looked Robert over and looked back at the men. Gary and Robert had been old friends, mostly of late competitive against one another. In the past they had been in several fistfights and drunken arguments about territorial things, but today they sat, listening to their fate.

"If you close Cadillac, we just come over around here to Creekville with the timber. It would just be a few more miles to run," Gary said as he shrugged off the mill closure.

The younger man smiled. "We are currently in negotiations with that mill now. It should be ours soon enough."

"Listen up, boys. The sad reality is here. The mills are coming to an end and it's all going to be small diameter boards. Hell, it already is. We are starting to get into some pretty heated environmental policies that none of us want, but the politicians need to get re-elected...just be prepared for the long commutes."

"Let us buy your land before it's too late - be good for us, be good for you," the young man said as he looked Robert over.

Robert put out his smoke in the ashtray and exhaled out his nose. "I don't think so."

"If we sell that land up there in Cadillac, we need your land. That is simply put. We need it and we will get it, you hear?" the old man stated, leaning forward and staring at Robert. Everyone paused. The older man continued, "You know as well as I do that none of you guys owns enough land not to take on contracts, and much of the private timbered land is a few years out to get logged again, especially in this portion of the county."

Smiling, Robert leaned in. "Take your faggot ass and go find some nigger dick to suck on."

"I am not from here and probably will not ever live in this state, "the quieter of the three said, as he folded his hands on one another, "but I can see what is happening all around here. It's obvious. I see things in dollar signs and the reality is that these farms here, the reason why you are starting to see some Mexican workers, is that they can work longer and harder than most white folks for half the price. Now, if you owned a farm and could get more work for half the price, wouldn't you take it?"

No one responded and he looked at everyone at the table. The mills that are tucked away in the middle of nowhere are not going to survive. Only a few mills will live to see another decade. Our Canadian neighbors to the north have all the big trees we could ever want, without the politics. It's all about money, boys. Your history is your history, and it may just be that."

Robert wiped his forehead and leaned back in his chair. "I have never lost a contract or made any mill poor."

Gary nodded. "Robert, I have heard about you all the way back east. They warned us that you may be difficult, that you may never give in to what we ask, may never give up, but how much do you need to lose before enough is enough?"

"Every goddamn bit a blood I got in my body! When my heart stops beating, you can run all over me, but until then I will keep bringing in the logs."

Robert picked himself up and laid down a ten-dollar bill. Gary watched his old friend get up, then followed his lead and dropped a few bills down on the table. The three men continued to sit, smiles on their faces.

"Be talking with you boys again, I'm sure," the older man said with a smirk, shaking his head.

Robert opened the exit door for Gary, who reached for his chew. "Never got to eat my food."

Robert smiled. "Me either. Let's go down the street and grab a burger."

Gary nodded as he hopped in Robert's truck.

"Never thought the day would come, Bob," Gary said, watching the passing buildings as they approached the burger stand.

"I know, but I can't just lay down because they ask me to. I just can't. It ain't in me, Gary."

"I know what you mean, but we think about the logistics of building roads and commuting, the wear and tear on the equipment, all the other small outfits around here grabbing contracts with starving hands…I don't know, Robert, my boy ain't going to see the wood we have."

"Yeah, probably right, pecker poles and needle dicks," Robert said as Gary laughed at his comment. The truck was parked and the two ordered burgers and sodas.

"Whatever happened to men doing the work, you know, from the top down, bottom up?" Gary asked as he looked around, finally focusing on Robert. "Society is changing, man. It's going to hell in a handbasket. Boys with long hair; women with short hair kissing one another; cocksuckers like those three back there telling me what to do…I got two hands and I plan on keep using them."

Robert paused and took a sip of his soda. "I bet they don't even wipe their own asses." Gary smiled and nodded as he finished his burger.

"Sounds like they are starting to get a few fires on the east side of the state. Guess a few folks are heading over there to help out cutting," Robert said and Gary agreed.

"Yeah, I will probably send a few folks that way just so they can make some money. Things are slowing down for us now."

Robert finished his burger. "You ready?" Gary nodded and two men walked stiffly toward the truck. The cab was hot. The midday sun had found itself high in the sky, without any clouds, just a sobering heat. Robert drove Gary to his truck and headed home.

26

Annie had paced around the house, doing some minor cleaning and chores, then left to have lunch with Susie. She talked to herself as she drove into town, continuing to question her desires and thoughts. It had been several months now since she and Billy had found their forgotten love, but day to day it was wearing her down. They rarely spoke much about the future and for the most part, both were content with their lives. But Annie wanted more, and was longing for more than just the volunteer work. She hoped she would get a call about the law work she put in for a short time ago. Pulling into the café, she smiled at Susie, who already had a window booth.

"Hello, how are you?" Annie asked as she greeted Susie, who accepted Annie's hug. The fan blew her hair against her face, and she tied it behind her head. Both of them were tired and their smiles did not mask their fatigue. The air was warm, and the ice tea they ordered cooled down some of their uncertainties and discomfort.

Annie stared out the window, watching the cars drift by slowly in the summer's heat as she listened to Susie complain about her kids and her husband, the school and the school board. She often left the conversation with wandering thoughts about her confusions. Susie picked up on this rather quickly and the two had a casual, meaningless conversation.

The check came and Annie offered to pay. Susie accepted, then asked her friend, "Are you okay?"

"I'm not sure. I'm not sure about much anymore."

Susie squinted her eyes, displaying the best compassion she could. "Well, what are you going to do?"

"I don't know. I figured by now I would know, but I don't," Annie said as she placed a few bills down on the check. The two hugged and walked outside into the heat.

"You call me, okay?" Susie said as she headed for her car.

"I will," Annie said as she hoped into the truck.

The air was warm, and she drove slowly through town and back out to Billy's place. She spent as much time taking hair out of her face as she did paying attention to the road. The trees provided some shade as she wove along the winding road. She pondered and mumbled to herself about her situation, about getting her own place so that Billy could slowly separate himself from his work and family ties, but questioned if that was what she really wanted, or what Billy really wanted. *What do I want? Where do I want to be? I'm getting old. Something needs to change; something needs to happen for me to commit to something. Do I really want to practice law in Dallas? Do I want to sit there straight faced and defend someone I know is guilty; all those perverts and violent fuckers, wife beaters and robbers?*

She found herself at Billy's house. She frowned when she realized Robert was home, his truck parked as if it had come to a sudden stop with the gravel moved, exposing the bare soil. She turned the key off, not knowing where else to go, and felt helpless, hoping that Billy would get off early so that she could at least throw her arms around him and hold him, squeeze out her frustrations on him.

The front door was open and she could see Robert pacing around the living room. "Hello, Robert, how are you?"

"Fucking pissed off - those bastards I met with are going to fuck us!"

Annie threw her purse down on the coffee table and took a seat, watching Robert pace around the kitchen, carrying a beer in his hand, sweat beading on his forehead. Annie let the silence speak for itself, watching as Robert lit a cigarette, exhaled and glanced at Annie. "Those fuckers want to play hardball. They are going to buy the mill in Creekville, probably to close them down so they can send all the wood down the road to Albany, 'n they basically said that Cadillac is done."

"They told you this?" Annie asked as she rested her head against the couch, lifting her feet and setting them on the coffee table. Robert nodded and stood up.

"My family has done this work for a hundred years, through thick and thin, good times and hard times, through several wars and bad years. Nothing shut us down or stood in our way." He bit his lip in frustration. Most people knew these times were near, but no one wanted to accept it.

"Who were these people?" Annie asked.

Robert looked at her and walked toward his chair and sat down. "They were some rich city boys making the decisions for the company. Never got their title or nothing, but they are the ones making the calls. Cocky fuckers, too." He shook his head once, took a long sip from his can, followed by a long drag from his smoke. "Not sure what their plan is, but they want my land and Gary's land that borders and intersects theirs. Probably going to sell it to another company or the government, or something or other."

Annie nodded. "What are you going to do?"

Robert jerked his head back in response. "Keep logging, keep cutting and hauling, giving my guys a reason to believe in something. As much as some of them hate it, hate me, they like doing it for the most part, and it's good money."

Annie nodded and remained silent. Robert looked her over, setting down his empty can. "You going to take my boy away from me?"

Annie was caught off guard and glanced at Robert, who looked at her with concern. "No, I don't think so," Annie said without much thought.

"You were the best thing that happened to him, still are."

There was a silence as the two stared out the window and watched as the trees and bushes gently danced in the afternoon breeze. "Part of me wants Billy to take on the family business and keep hitting it, raise a family and keep it going, 'n part of me wants to kick him in the ass and send him heading somewhere else."

Surprised at the openness, not knowing what to do or say, Annie looked at Robert, and gently rocked back and forth.

"You going to take care of him?" Robert asked as he bit his lip. "I got nothing left, Annie."

Her eyes began to water, a tear ran down her cheek and dropped on her blouse. She nodded in agreement, whispering, "Ya."

"Part of me wants to hang it up before I get forced to, and part of me wants to keep going, ride out these tough times and keep moving forward." Robert paused and glanced around the house. "Overcome plenty of hard times before; just easier to keep working than thinking about them, but it's hard. I see my wife everywhere I look in this house; I see my baby boy everywhere I go."

Robert paused again as he bit his lips with more force, not wanting to let go. Annie watched as tears ran down her cheeks. "Billy loves you. It's good to see," Robert said as he got up to go outside. Annie could no longer stop her tears and began to cry, letting herself go.

Leaning forward, she cried into her hands and rocked gently back and forth, picking herself up just as Hank entered the house. He quickly darted toward Annie and rested his paws on her knees to lick her tears. She laughed and tried to retreat, but the retriever would not give up. He jumped on her and continued to lick her hands and face, placing his paw on her legs as leverage. She heard a truck door slam shut and Billy shout something at his dad in frustration. Robert was in the shop and she heard something slam down.

Billy walked inside, frustration turning to a smile as he watched his dog wrestle with Annie, her face wet with licks and tears, smiles hiding her recent frowns. Billy set down his lunch pale and walked toward the fridge to grab a beer. "You want one?" Billy asked as he opened a can.

"Yes!" Annie screamed at Billy as she pushed Hank off her.

"I was asking the dog, but you want one, too?" Billy laughed as he brought her a beer, placing the can in her hand and a kiss on her lips, which she welcomed and needed.

Robert walked in for a briefing on today's events. "Well, how did it go today?"

Billy broke away his attention from Annie. "Fucking sucked. Yarder's engine went tits up; spent half the day fixing that, and the head gasket on Red's saw is shot." Robert shook his head as he walked to the fridge.

"Ah fuck!" Robert yelled, grabbing a beer. "Is the yarder working now?"

Billy watched as his dad struggled to open his beer. "Yeah, should be." Robert nodded and headed back outside.

"I thought about you a lot today," Billy said as he rubbed his warm hand down Annie's tan exposed leg.

"Me too. Sometimes I wish we could just lay around all day and do nothing."

Billy smiled and glanced outside. "Maybe after dinner we can do some of that laying around thing."

Annie smiled. "Once you start, you may not want to stop." Billy laughed in response and gave a slight slap on her thigh as he got up to get a refill.

27

Annie awoke early, before Billy, which was unusual. She headed to the bathroom. Her nipples burned, not like before, not like any time she could remember. Half asleep, she rested on the toilet, tired and dizzy, perplexed and slightly nauseated. She finished, got up, guided by the dark walls for support, her shirt irritating her nipples. She returned to bed and took the shirt off, still dizzy and feeling sick. Billy turned over, still asleep and threw his hand on her stomach, which was not pleasant for her. Annie lay still, concerned, uncomfortable and confused. She stared at the ceiling, feeling the early morning breeze find its way into the room from the open window.

She lifted her eyes when Billy placed a kiss on her lips. She smiled and watched as he walked out of the room for another day's work. The sun was just beginning to crest the eastern hills. She rolled over and her head rocked a little. She frowned and lay still. This same feeling had happened just a few days before, and she planned to head to Dallas to check out why. Her appointment was later that day.

Billy and Red organized the crew and finished another landing. The crew moved slowly in the summer heat, moving equipment and gear to another site. The day was young when Billy and Red escaped early to head down to the bar. Ray's Place was empty inside, just a few folks finding some shade and cold drinks. Robbie was there, and Billy gave him a slap on the shoulder. Red moved further down the bar to greet another friend.

"How the hell are you?" Robbie said to Billy, picking his head up from a book.

Billy nodded as he received a cold draft from Ray. "Whiskey, too," he said to Ray, who poured a tall shot. "All right I guess. Work is slowing down, 'n well, I don't know, Robbie, guess I'm at a crossroads."

"If you are at a crossroads, you got four roads to choose from. Well, really three, 'cause you can't go backwards, as much as some of us wish we could. But now here you sit, drink in hand, work and women sitting down these roads, which one you going to take, the high or low, the one that's easy or the one that's hard, the one you can see, or the one you can't?"

Billy listened, grabbed the shot and threw it back, the whiskey warm and burning a little as it found its way to his stomach. Robbie set his book down. "Life is funny, ain't it?"

Billy nodded in response. He enjoyed listening to Robbie talk, as it provided a different flavor of thought than he was used to.

"What's on your mind, kid?"

"Work and women, what else?"

"Listen up, Billy. I don't know much, but I know with each passing second life allows the possibilities of change. It's just taking advantage of that gift and running with it, that's all. See, change is inevitable, is the only true thing that stays the same. Don't matter who you are or where you're at, or what you think or don't; the only thing that stays the same is change."

Billy listened and watched Robbie take a deep sip of beer, leaving some of its foam on his thick mustache.

"You read a lot?" Billy asked as he gazed at the Hemingway novel.

"Yes, I do. It's my escape. That and the beer and the occasional joint, but I like it. Brings me some calmness and makes me think and ponder; breaks up the boredom and predictability. You know I can travel for thousands of miles in a book without moving not more than a few feet."

Billy watched as Robbie lit another smoke. "Why don't you log anymore?"

Robbie turned toward Billy. "I never much cared for it. I mean, it was good work, but the thing is with work like that, it will build you up when you are young and break you down when you get old."

Billy nodded. If it was not the work that broke his friends down, it was the bottle or something else that got in the way. The two sat silently, watching as the door opened and more folks arrived from the crew and elsewhere. Billy nodded at his co-workers and friends who came in, but he continued to ponder Robbie's words. Robbie tilted his glass back and grabbed his book, getting up and slapping Billy on the shoulder. "Take care of yourself and be careful, for Christ's sake."

Billy smiled. "All right, better get out of here before she has to come down here and drag your ass home."

Robbie smiled. "Sometimes even us old dogs can learn new tricks. Listen, things will work themselves out the way they're supposed to. They always do, even when you least expect it." Billy nodded and watched Robbie push the door open, allowing some of the sunlight to enter the dark tavern.

28

"Annie Sutton?" A blonde-haired, young nurse asked as she gazed around the waiting room at the doctor's office. Annie got up and walked toward the nurse, who pointed her toward the scale. The nurse began to chart her height and weight, and then guided her into the examining room, took her vitals and smiled. "The doctor will be right with you."

Minutes passed as she glanced at the wall and read through various pamphlets regarding symptoms and information on every disease and condition known to mass media. Much of the information frightened her once she could place her symptoms with those of many of the diseases and cancers described. Her thoughts were interrupted by the doctor entering the room, staring at the empty chart.

"Hello, I'm Dr. Brown," he said with a smile.

"I'm Annie," she said, looking down on the rather short doctor who was beginning to bald and show his age.

"So you are here, complaining of nausea and dizziness, etc."

Annie nodded as he set down his clipboard and asked her to lie down.

She hesitated, then leaned back. "Are you sexually active?" Annie nodded and whispered, "Yes."

The doctor gently palpated her stomach and stood back. Annie looked at him as he stared at her hand. "Well, the conditions seem to me that you are most likely pregnant. A few simple tests will reveal that, and we can let you know as soon as tomorrow."

Annie nodded with concern.

"Are you experiencing any other pain or any other symptoms?" Annie shook her said and cleared her throat.

"No, just the ones I told you."

"Well, you seem really healthy and if I had to guess, I would say that would be the first place we should look, and then go from there." The doctor picked up the clipboard and noted a few things. "I will show you to the nurse and she can take some blood and urine samples."

"Okay, thank you." Annie said as she walked toward the nurse, who welcomed her with a smile.

The nurse was gentle as she poked Annie's arm with a needle and took some blood, causing Annie to get a little dizzy in response. The nurse then guided Annie toward the bathroom to fill a cup for analysis. Annie finished and left, and the nurse explained that they would know the results soon and would contact her as soon as they could.

The sun welcomed Annie as the late afternoon heated the asphalt and concrete around the town. She opened the truck door and rolled down the window, trying to start the rig quickly and get some breeze rolling through the cab. She grabbed her purse and found her cigarettes, placed a smoke in her mouth and caught herself in the mirror. She sat motionless, staring at herself, took the smoke out and set it back in the pack.

She drove nervously out of town toward the country roads that led back to Hemlock. A Dolly Parton song echoed from the truck radio and Annie sang along, battling the curves and tears, the lyrics guiding her way, guiding her thoughts and travels.

29

Billy tried his damnedest to concentrate on the pool game, but too many things raced through his mind. His father's worries, Annie's uncertainties, and his own possibilities plagued his scattered thoughts. He threw the stick against the balls, crackling as they shot into the pockets and before too long, the game was over and he was surprised that he ran through his balls more quickly than expected. He smiled at the choker boy. "Keep practicing there, kid."

"You ain't any better of a pool player than you are a worker," Red shouted at the younger kid. The folks who heard the comment laughed as Billy nodded to the other kid and handed him the stick. The boy smirked as he grabbed the stick and began talking shit to his friend. They argued a bit as Billy returned to his bar stool. Robert had entered the bar and greeted a few folks before sitting next to Billy.

"How did it go today?" he asked, coughing as he took a large sip and focused on his boy.

"We moved to the other site, but hit shutdown so we left early," Billy said as he looked back at his dad, eyes glazed, showing their time in the tavern.

Robert nodded. "Where's Annie?"

Billy reached for one of his father's cigarettes. "She should be down here soon enough. Had a few errands to run, I think." Robert nodded as he reached into a nearby bowl and grabbed some peanuts. The two sat comfortably silent. Billy looked into the mirror where their eyes met. Billy lowered his head.

"I think I may take her to the coast this weekend. Been a long time since I smelled the ocean and ate some chowder."

"Well, that would be nice. Been a long time since I went. A few years since we went fishing down there, ain't it?"

Billy nodded in response. "Yeah, too long ago."

"Listen, take good care of that gal. The good ones don't just come and go with the breeze."

Billy nodded. "Will do."

"I'm fucking serious, boy. The good ones you need to keep close at hand," Robert said. Billy nodded again and took a drag from the smoke. "Don't just shake your head like I am talking about work or sports or something. Don't fuck this one up, you hear?"

"Jesus, I get it. Don't plan on it, okay, Pops?" There eyes met long enough to feel each other's sincerity.

Ray turned the TV on and flipped it to a baseball game. The two McDonoughs were content watching the slow-paced game, sipping their beers, waiting for something to happen. Billy would eagerly glance at the door whenever it opened, waiting to see Annie walk in. Occasionally, as the minutes passed, they would get into friendly arguments about women, sports or work with their visiting friends. The hours began to pass by slowly, like so many other similar days and weeks, months and years.

30

Annie drove fast along the rural highways, dodging as the setting sun shone bright against her eyes. Her mind was cluttered with confusion and possibilities. She felt impatient, nervously wanting to see Billy, more so than usual—just to see him, his eyes and smile and calming touch. He was the only one she'd told about going to the doctor; her mother still drowning with work and scotch, too far removed for love or kindness. Susie had been an enjoyable acquaintance since her return to Hemlock, but even their discussions were more vague and meaningless than she had hoped for.

Her thoughts switched back to the highway as her truck approached the town limits of Hemlock. She eased upon the gas pedal and found a more reasonable pace. Turning down the music, she rested her arm along the open window. Dusk was setting in, but the air was still crisp and warm. Slowing down to see if Billy's truck was parked at Ray's Place, she shook her head. She drove in, parked next to his truck and turned the engine off. She sat looking at herself in the rearview mirror. She checked her eyes and the faint lines that had recently developed, slowly exposing her age. The phone call did not need to take place - she felt different; something was happening to her body.

She caressed the steering wheel, gripping it with both hands and gently rubbing it before she picked her head up and opened the door. She paused, not knowing whether she felt happy or sad, certainly confused, probably just scared. Forcing a smile at a passing stranger, she dragged herself out of the truck and listened as her feet grazed through the gravel parking lot to the front door of the tavern.

Opening the door, she found Billy arguing with Lee and waited for a break in the conversation before she showed herself to Billy.

"You mean to tell me that the fucking Raiders are better then the Steelers?" Lee yelled at Billy after glancing at Annie.

Billy's back was at Annie. "Damn straight," Billy said, nodding and smiling.

"Get the fuck outta here," Lee said as he turned away from Billy in disgust. Billy stared ahead at the bar until he realized Annie was standing just beside him. He smiled and threw his arm around her. She gently kissed him and separated herself from his grip long enough to smile and ask how he was. It was apparent he had been there awhile and she was upset about it, but did not show it. She sat down next to him as Ray brought her a beer. She stared at it for a second and pushed it away. Billy noticed.

"How was your trip to Dallas? You all right?"

"I will be; just tired and worn down. I'm not feeling all that well, babe," she said as she turned toward him and rested her head on her hand. Billy nodded and gave her his attention.

"You want to go then, probably?" Annie nodded as she laid her head down and looked at Billy. He stood up and shot his beer back, leaned back and stumbled slightly. Annie watched. It was a familiar scene, one she had accepted, but that at times dragged her down. She picked up her head, sat up straight and stretched before getting off the bar stool.

She smiled at Billy. "If you want to stay, please do. I will be fine." Smirking, Billy knew better than to take the bait.

"Nah, I would rather be with you than in here." Annie lifted her eyebrows in response.

As they walked outside, Billy grabbed her close and put his arm around her shoulders. She rested her head on his arm as they staggered toward their trucks. He walked her to hers. "I'll see you at home."

Annie nodded and watched as Billy walked around her truck towards his. "Hey!" Annie yelled at Billy, who stopped and rested his arms on her truck. "What about us going and getting our own place?"

Billy paused, somewhat perplexed. "Tonight?"

Annie laughed and shook her head. "No. I mean, do you want to go look sometime soon for our own place?"

Billy laughed and agreed without saying much, other than, "Sure."

He lifted his arms off her truck and walked a couple more steps toward his, stopping to look back. Annie had not moved. He glanced at her. "You want to go to the coast?"

Annie arched her back and smiled. "Now?"

Billy laughed. "Not tonight, but maybe tomorrow."

Annie smiled in anticipation. "I'd love to."

Billy smiled back. "Okay, let's go home."

Annie started the truck. She looked back and Billy had already skidded off down the road.

She tried to catch him but never did see his taillights until she entered the driveway. He was opening the front door when she pulled in. Hank greeted her as she opened the truck door. Smiling at the dog, she slapped his head with some friendly pets as she walked toward the house. Hank darted off after smelling a squirrel. Annie walked into the house and Billy handed her some leftover pizza. She was surprised and gladly accepted the slice, then watched Billy rip through several pieces before she finished hers. He washed it down with a tall glass of water and burped with pleasure. She shook her head, laughing, but also secretly fearful.

"You ready for bed?" he asked as he leaned against his doorway for support. Annie nodded and walked to him, placing her lips on his as he leaned forward. She helped him toward the bed, then unbuttoned his pants and slid them off as his eyes were closed and lost, reaching with his hand, trying to grab whatever part of her he could. She dodged his attempts until he got hold of her. She sat on his waist and took off her shirt and bra. He grabbed her hips, tilted his head back and smiled. She sat motionless, waiting to see if he would eventually fall asleep, which he did after a minute or two. She gently lifted herself off him and took off the rest of her clothes. She fell asleep to his soft snores.

31

     Billy awoke early. He always had a hard time sleeping in; never did. Since he was just a boy, his father always had something for him to do, so sleep was rarely an option. Today lacked the work, but the routine of an early rise was no different. He rolled over to find Annie's back. He rested his hand on her hips and began to gently message her lower back and exposed legs. She was still asleep, but sensed the attack and moved away from him. He tried again, grabbing her hips, dragging her closer. She resisted again and moved forward. Giving up, he got out of bed and threw on some clothes.

     Hank greeted him outside his room and Billy handed the dog a few cups of food in his plate. The dog smelled the food and moved away, then gestured the need to go outside. Billy opened the door to find it still dark outside. He rubbed his forehead, trying to release the heaviness and tension that weighed on his mind. He blinked hard a few times and tried to wipe the sleep from his eyes. Pouring water into the coffee pot, he sat still listening to the coffee pot slowly brew.

     Normally, Robert would be up by now. Billy turned the porch light on outside and looked to see if his dad had made it home last night, but it did not look that way. Sometimes Ray would hide his dad's keys and make him stay the night at the bar. There was a room out back with a few small beds that usually the drunkest person at the bar found himself in for the night. Billy shut the light off as Hank returned to the house.

     Billy walked toward the kitchen, cursing as he banged his shoulder into the open doorway. The coffee was dark and black as he poured it into his coffee mug. He waited momentarily before sipping it. Opening the fridge, he stared at the shelves over and over again as if there was some meaningful message inside. He shut the door and walked away to grab a cooking pan.

"Gonna cook my girl a meal," he mumbled as he trotted around the kitchen in circles trying to find materials and ingredients.

Annie rolled over to an empty bed, lifted her head briefly and caught a smell of food from the kitchen. She got up and began to slowly dress. She walked quietly outside the bedroom and toward the kitchen. Hank lifted his head to greet her as Annie placed her hand on his head and whispered for him to be quiet. She stopped just short of the kitchen and leaned against the wall, watching as Billy darted around the kitchen, throwing drawers closed, then opening the fridge and closing it without grabbing or putting back anything. Annie laughed as she watched the display and eventually interrupted his cooking concentration. "What are you making?"

"The whole nine yards, babe," he said in response, pausing and then walked toward her to place a kiss on her lips. The kiss was louder than usual, causing Annie to chuckle and wipe her mouth. Flavoring the potatoes with a healthy dose of pepper, he said, "Sorry about last night."

"You did not do anything wrong," she said as she walked by him and slapped him on the ass. Reaching for a cup, she poured herself a healthy dose of coffee.

"Go sit down or something. I was going to bring you breakfast in bed."

Annie looked at the creation and smiled. "All right." She went into the living room and began reading the previous day's paper. She was beginning to read through the front page when Billy placed a plate of food in front of her.

"It's the McDonough mix." Billy nodded proudly as he began to devour his plate of food. Annie hesitated momentarily, smiling as she lifted her fork and poked at the food. Surprisingly, the food tasted good, and she found herself finishing the whole plate. Billy watched and waited for approval. "Well, what do you think?"

She wiped her mouth with her hand and smiled. "It was really quite good, Billy."

He picked up her plate and placed it with his in the sink, then massaged his stomach with pleasure. The sun was rising and Billy walked outside to take a piss. Hank followed and sniffed his way into the brush to search for critters. Annie watched from inside, weighed down after eating too much, then returned to the couch to read the paper. Billy found an ax and began tossing it against a large bull's eye that he and his dad set up a few years back. He raised the ax over his head and tossed it over and over against the target, sticking the blade into the wood with accuracy and precision. It had been a few years since he had entered any logging competitions. The McDonoughs historically did well, but of late, they were absent from the competition. A few years back, Robert threatened the judges when he felt Boone got screwed on one of the competitions, so Robert never returned and Billy never really cared much for it. After a few minutes, Billy left the resting ax against the target and walked back inside.

"Well, should we go to the coast today or what?" he asked as he sat down next to Annie.

"Sure, I have nothing better to do."

"Okay, I will call a guy I know over there in Newport and let him know we are heading that way. He should have a place for us to stay." He left her alone with the newspaper, walked out to his truck and began unloading his gear into the shed. He started prepping for a road trip, grabbing the ice chest and tarp, sleeping bags and shotgun.

The phone rang; Annie got up and picked it up. Billy was walking back inside when he saw Annie on the phone. He paused and wondered if it was for him, but she had her back to him and was talking quietly. He walked into his room, grabbed a bag and threw some clothes into it, then put it over his shoulder and walked back to the living room.

Annie stood motionless, staring at Billy, frozen in fright and concern. Billy stopped and set down his bag, waiting for a response.

"That was the doctor. I'm pregnant."

Billy leaned back against the wall and stared at the ground, lifting his head to set his eyes on hers. She let her head drop. He walked toward her and rested his arms around her back and held her close. She picked her arms up and wrapped them around him. "Well, I guess that changes things, eh?" Billy said as he separated himself.

Annie was fighting joy with sadness, comfort with uncertainty. "I think it can be good, right?" she said as she wiped a few tears from her eyes. Billy smiled, not knowing what to do or say, not knowing if he wanted kids, not knowing much about much.

"Yeah, we can make it work."

She walked back over to Billy. "Please hug me." Billy stood straight up. Any hangover he may have had was long gone; his mind crystal clear with fear and confusion. Annie began to cry, competing with the songbirds outside and the slow, calming sounds of the nearby creek. He tried to breathe quietly as she wiped her face against his shirt.

"There is nothing to worry about," Billy said in a calming whisper. It was a voice that Annie had never heard before, causing her to lift her face and place a kiss on his lips. He tried to smile; she did the same.

Their eyes met, trying to read each other's thoughts, trying to maintain some civility and sobriety. Too many images racing through each other's mind, too many possibilities rocking their stabilities. Billy walked away toward his bag and stared at it, lifting his head to look at a family photo where he and his brothers stood, young in age, his mom's arms wrapped around them. Annie watched Billy from across the room as she took a seat on a chair, leaning forward, nervous. The silence was becoming difficult for both of them.

Billy turned back toward Annie. "Well, should we go to the coast?"

Annie smiled and cleared her throat. "I guess we should."

Billy nodded, grabbing his bag. "Waiting on you," he said, opening the door and heading for the truck.

Annie smiled nervously and continued to sit, slowly rocking back and forth. Billy returned a minute later and headed to the kitchen to pour himself another cup of coffee. Annie watched him, studying his build and stature, dimensions and stance. He turned back toward her.

"How long you want to go for?"

Billy shrugged his shoulders. "I'd say a night or two."

Annie nodded with approval and went off to pack a few things for the road trip. Billy walked to the windows in the living room that provided the view of the creek and woods. He stared out, scanning the forest floor. The news hit him pretty hard. His careless ways needed to change; his approach forever altered; his mind heavy again with thought.

He walked outside and started the truck, listening to the motor cough a bit and idle. Annie walked outside. Billy watched as Annie flung her hair behind her as the morning breeze picked it up. She threw a small backpack in the truck. "I left a note for your father saying we would be back in a day or two."

Billy nodded and said, "Hell, he don't give a shit."

Annie smiled. "I think he does," she said.

32

Robert stumbled home to find an empty house. His head and body ached after a long day and night of drinking. He cleared his throat and reached for a glass of water. He could feel his heartbeat pound against his forehead. Looking down on the table, he saw a note written by Annie. He tried to read, pushing the page further away in order to see well, his eyes fading faster than the rest of his weary body. Shaking his head, he smiled, muttering, "Damn boy is pussy-whipped."

He set down the page and looked at Hank, who sat wagging his tail, waiting for something to happen. "Not today, boy. This old man is hurting pretty good." The dog grabbed a bone and walked it over to the couch where Robert followed. The afternoon sun was trying to shine through the trees. Robert ignored the heat the best he could as he took off his boots and lay down on the couch.

Hank licked Robert in the face and the old man moved back, smiling at the dog. He slapped his hand on Hank's head and got up, grunting, to feed the dog. Watching as Hank ate his food, Robert walked to the fridge and scanned it for dinner. He found deli meat that he whipped up into a quick sandwich and walked around the house as he ate, pondering whether he should head back to town. The sun was setting and he felt tired, so he returned to the couch and turned on the television.

Nothing seemed entertaining, and he turned the set off and grabbed the paper. Hank returned to rest by his feet. Robert leaned over, slapped the dog a few times and smiled. "Guess it's just you and me tonight." The dog lifted his head in approval before lowering it to the ground, exhaling with a grunt. Robert smiled and lay back down on the couch, listening to the quiet sounds that dusk provided: the buzz from the refrigerator, the dog's snores, the living room clock ticking and the early evening breeze hitting the wind chimes outside. He lay staring at the ceiling, trying to relax and breathe. Trying not to think about the mills closing or his crew, their equipment, or Billy. Trying not to think about the day Boone died or the day his wife fell forever asleep. A lump grew in his throat, pressure built in his face, his nose was ready to run, his eyes ready to water. He shook his head and closed his eyes, listening to the rhythm of the night.

33

The truck was heading west on the Territorial Creek Road, which followed the creek, weaving its way through the scenic and winding watercourse. Annie looked at a road map of the route and saw that while it appeared to be a shortcut, the condition of the road actually made it a longer route. The road was abused by equipment, logging trucks and occasional hikers and campers used it for access, but rarely anyone drove it to get to the other side of the Coast Range. The truck bounced and shook as it hit washboard bumps and potholes along its gravel existence.

Annie was beginning to feel ill, as if she had been riding an old lawn mover for the last 30 minutes. She tried to remain patient, but was frustrated. "Why did we take this route?"

Billy lit a smoke and looked at Annie. "I like this road. No traffic and it's pretty out here, plus I get to watch your tits bounce along the way."

Annie looked down and shook her head, and then slapped Billy in the arm and smiled. She gazed outside and watched the creek move its way west. The hillsides were diverse with various trees of varying age. "See over there around this bend here? There is an old wigwam. My grandfather use to log here and there was a big camp."

Annie nodded as she saw the old structure faded by years and undergrowth standing along some flats just below the hillside. "And you see that trail-like thing running on the other side of the creek?" Annie nodded. "That was the old tracks that they shipped the logs down, all the way to the coast." The truck entered another set of washboards and Billy glanced down at Annie's breasts.

She noticed. "You pig," she said.

Billy shrugged his shoulders as he put out his smoke. "Pavement is just up ahead."

Her mind began to wander as she listened to the radio. Billy remained quiet as he nodded with the music. Various images raced through her mind, causing her to shake her head with concern. *What am I going to do? Where am I going to live? Does Billy really want this kid?* She glanced over at Billy, who was lost in driving and music. She took a deep breath and watched as the pavement provided a few more country homes to gaze at.

The two remained silent, both thinking, both scared, both trying to distract their minds with thoughts other than the news they had heard that morning. Billy did not want to address the issue, but wanted to let things work themselves out. Annie wanted some clarity and answers to her lingering questions. Instead, the truck found its way to the main highway just a few miles short of the ocean. The air was changing, thicker than before, cooling down the cab, and Annie rolled up part of her window.

They were reaching the city limits high on the last hill that overlooked the ocean and town below them. Annie watched the last of the trees and brush turn to homes and city streets. A sign caught her eye along the side of the road that caused her to laugh. She recited it to Billy. "Someone placed a sign high up in a tree saying, 'Go home California.'" Billy laughed, trying to look back at the sign. Annie waited impatiently to see the ocean.

Billy took the first left at the streetlight and took the truck down toward the bayfront. Crab pots stood piled high, lining the streets for hundreds of feet. The seagulls glided in the sea breeze, perching themselves high on the fishing boats. The bay bridge crested tall in the sky and sea lions barked. Annie smiled and leaned back in the seat, watching as tourists walked up and down the busy streets. Dock workers dodged careless drivers and walkers. The sun was out, shedding warmth when blocked by the wind, but the sea breeze created a cooler air than they were used to.

Billy spied an old fishermen's tavern. "Lets grab a beer, eh?"

Annie darted a look at Billy, frustrated. "How about we go walk on the beach first?" Billy shrugged in agreement as he watched the tavern go by and continued down through the bayfront.

They stopped high on a hill that overlooked the jetties and ocean, and spotted a trail. They began to walk through the shore pines and dunes to the beach. Once in the sand, Annie took off her sandals and carried them as she dragged her toes through the cool sand. Billy followed Annie's lead, took off his shoes and studied his bleach- white toes, cluttered with boot marks and calluses.

A few kites filled the late morning sky and dogs ran free along the beach. The tide was low, exposing miles and miles of open sand and drift logs. They walked without distraction, the ocean echoing its presence. Annie led the way to the water's edge, and ran back and forth with the incoming tides, as she had as a child, laughing and dancing around. Billy watched from a few dozen yards away, admiring her hair pushed around her face, her teeth exposed in laughter.

She was wearing herself out as Billy stood watching the distant boats on the horizon, the sea mist cooling his head. Annie ran toward Billy and jumped on him, throwing her hand around his neck, placing her lips on his. He fell back slightly, trying to regain his balance, dropped his shoes, grabbed her butt and held her up. He began spinning her around and around until he was too dizzy and fell over into the sand, causing Annie to yell with excitement. Breathless, they lay down, her hair dancing around her face, sand blowing against their eyes. Squinting, the two rolled over and sat, grabbing each other and wrestling.

Billy stood and grabbed her hand to help her up. They began to walk back toward the trail, but Billy scooped her up and threw her over his shoulder, as if he were hiking with his saw. She began beating his back and shouting at him as he marched along smiling, tapping her butt with his other hand. She leaned further down and began slapping his butt. He set her on her feet. She punched his chest, turned away and started jogging in front of him. He watched her prance around without a care or concern.

They found the trail and walked slowly uphill until they could see the bay and the incoming fishing boats heading from the ocean between the two rocky jetties. "Look at all those seagulls following the fishing boat," Annie said, trying to catch her breath.

Billy smiled. "I bet they get shit on quite a bit."

Losing interest, Billy grabbed his keys and turned to Annie. "Let's grab some food; I'm fucking starving." Annie agreed and followed him to the truck. They drove down a few side streets until they approached another old part of town where they spotted a chowder house. Inside, the place was cozy with fishing memorabilia. They indulged in chowder and garlic bread. The food was warm and satisfying. Billy paid, and the two got up and walked slowly to the door.

Outside the fog was beginning to move in, the sun still perched its rays to the eastern hillsides, but the west was blocked by a bank of gray. They headed down the street toward the beach again and found a bench to rest. Billy watched waves come and go, as Annie leaned against him and closed her eyes. They chatted a little bit, but mostly small talk about the ocean and food. Not much about the kid on the way or where they might end up. Instead, they let the sea breeze cleanse their thoughts, cooling down their uncertainties and calming their wandering minds.

Annie broke the silence. "Are you going to call your friend?"

Billy stopped squinting and looked at Annie. "Yeah, I should." He looked around and spotted a pay phone. "I'll be back in a second."

Annie crossed her legs on the bench, watching as Billy walked across the street toward the phone. A family pulled a car up between her and Billy. The car was packed with three kids of varying ages, with their parents wide-eyed and stressed. The mother got out of the car, yelling at the oldest to behave, grabbed the younger boy and helped him out of the car. The older kid was carrying a football and pushing his other brother. The father exited the car, distancing himself from the family as he scanned the surroundings. The mother was angry, pointing at her kid. Annie shook her head. "Fuck, I hope that's not what I have to look forward to."

Billy returned minutes later to see Annie shaking her head, still watching the family argue and walk toward the beach. "What's wrong?" Billy asked as he sat back down and followed Annie's eyes to the family. Annie turned to Billy and caught his eyes.

"Promise me we won't turn into that."

Billy laughed as he assessed the family. Shaking his head, he said, "Don't plan on it, babe."

Annie rested her head against his chest again as he wrapped his arm around her shoulder. "Was Chris home?"

"Yeah, he said he would meet us down here at the bar near the chowder house in an hour."

Annie nodded in agreement. "Have you seen him since high school?"

Billy lifted his chest slightly to regain a more comfortable seat. "Once, I think, a few years back at the county fair. He came down to flick us shit for the loggers competition." Billy laughed. "I remember, fuck that's right, we all ended up at Ray's Place. It was fucking packed, lots of girls, and he ended up hooking up with, god what's her name, she was a few years younger than us, big girl...anyways, god she was ugly. Last time I saw him was with his arm around her, kissing her neck. We were all laughing our asses off."

Billy started laughing and laughing, uncontrollably, to the point he started coughing and pushing Annie aside. She couldn't help but laugh, too. "Ah fuck, I got to remind him of that. Every time I see that girl, I bust out laughing." He wiped a few tears from his eyes and reached for a cigarette.

Annie stood up and stretched, smiling at Billy's story. "Let's head up to the tavern then. I could use some tea or juice."

Billy coughed and nodded with a smile, still thinking back to that night several years ago. Clearing his throat he said, "Okay, let's do it."

The tavern was dark with tables spread across the floor in a disorganized way, bar stools worn down from years of visitors. Music played loudly in the almost empty bar. The bartender was smoking and nodded at the two when they took their seats at the bar.

"What will it be?" the lady asked as she inhaled her smoke. Billy looked at Annie, who asked for orange juice.

Billy gestured for whatever was on tap. The lady nodded. "Honey, did you want some vodka in that OJ?"

Annie lifted her head to listen to the question. "No thanks," she said. The lady looked surprised, but followed the requests. The beer was cold and delicious, and Billy swallowed two large gulps in a quick fashion, leaving some foam on his lips. Annie sipped her orange juice with some frustration, but acceptance.

The two sat there, minding their own business, commenting on the tavern and their day so far. A few folks entered the bar. They looked like locals, mostly fishermen. At one point, a tourist walked in wearing a Hawaiian shirt and stopped a few feet in to look around, then cast a concerned smile before making a quick exit. With everyone watching, the bartender quietly commented, "Do you think he was lost?"

Billy smiled, feeling at home. The dark confines of a tavern could be anywhere in the state – hell, the country for that matter, and be home to him. Most folk who frequent its walls can find some harmony and comfort. The drinks taste the same; the scenery is similar. Many folks would shy away from these walls, not just here, but many of the dark walls throughout the country and beyond. There is no need to glorify the sin or behavior that takes place, sparked by drink and conversation, but it can serve as a place of comfort for some. Its walls serve a place for retreat and praise, similar to a place of worship in a different context and light. He lifted his head to read a quote: "Home is where the drink is." He laughed and pointed it out to Annie, who smiled and shook her head at it.

The door flung open and Chris walked in. Billy turned on his bar stool and got up. "Oh shit, how the hell are you?"

Chris smiled at Billy. "Pretty fucking good." The two collided for a handshake and a slap on the shoulder, each trying to squeeze the other's hand into submission. "Fuck, you looking big, dude," Chris said.

"Working man, just lots of time working," Billy said, then introduced Annie.

"Yeah, I know the feeling," Chris said in response. "Annie, that's you! I heard you were a lawyer in Seattle."

Annie took a sip of her juice. "I was until recently."

Chris nodded at the bartender, who was way ahead of him, delivering the beer without hesitation. "So, what's up with you two, back together again?" Billy and Annie smiled at each other and gave similar nods. "Wow, shit, well it was probably meant to be," he said as he found a barstool next to Billy.

"You staying busy?" Billy asked as he ordered another round for the two of them. "Fuck yeah, salmon in the summer, crabbing in the winter." Billy nodded in approval. "How about you? How's your family doing?"

Billy leaned back, wiped the leftover beer from his lips and looked at Annie. Chris waited for a response and realized something had changed. Billy cleared his throat. "Well, Mom and Boone died this past winter," he said, then paused while Chris studied his face. "Mom got cancer and Boone got caught on the hill 'n crushed." Billy arched his back and took another sip. Annie placed her hand on his lower back. The silence was thick. Billy massaged his trigger hand to calm his nerves.

"I had no fucking clue, Billy. I'm sorry. How is your dad holding up?"

Billy shook his head, took another sip, lit a smoke and looked into Chris' eyes. "He's all right; getting older and meaner; under some stress with the mills likely to close down near us."

Chris leaned back and watched as his friend inhaled the smoke. He grabbed a smoke from his pack and lit it, exhaling, waiting for a change in the conversation. Billy chuckled. "I was telling Annie about the last time I saw you, and we ended up at the tavern and you went home with that big girl." Chris exhaled and laughed, causing him to cough and take a long sip of beer.

"Yeah, Liz; she was a handful."

Annie shook her head. "You guys are assholes. She was a nice girl." Billy held back and looked at Chris, and they broke into laughter again.

"Yeah, she was pretty nice." Billy laughed again at Chris, who shook his head.

"You guys got a place to stay tonight?" Chris asked as he put his smoke out in the ashtray.

"Hoping to stay at your place," Billy said as he looked at Chris.

He nodded in agreement. "Yeah, my roommate is gone fishing for a bit, 'n I got to leave in the morning for another trip. It's all yours if you want it."

Annie thanked him and Billy put his smoke out. "Probably just be for the night," he said, looking at Annie, who agreed.

They sat and drank for a few hours until they couldn't take the band's music anymore. They walked out and headed up the hill toward the house, laughing about old times and continuing on about high school and beyond. As they walked in, Chris showed them to their room, and Annie began to take her shoes off and lie down.

"You want a beer, Billy?"

Billy looked down at Annie. "Yeah, sure."

Annie smiled back at Billy. "Go on, have some fun. I'm tired. Come to bed soon." Billy gave her a kiss as he left the room to talk with Chris.

Annie could make out some of their conversations from the living room as they talked about life, women and work. Chris went on about fishing and Billy responded with logging. Both expressed interest in, and respect for, each other's occupation. Eventually, Chris ended the conversation after he realized he needed to be at the boat in just a few hours. They collided for a last handshake and went their separate ways. Billy entered the room and accidentally woke up Annie, who welcomed him with open arms and exposed skin. Billy admired her body and quickly pushed himself against her naked skin.

They lay together, whispering about their day. The waves crashed against the nearby shore. The winds occasionally picked up and shook the house a bit, but the constant song of the waves created a peaceful tone to their sleep. Before long the two were fast asleep, dreaming their dreams of hope and fear.

34

Robert awoke early to Hank's licking his hand just before the morning light. It had been Robert's first sober night's sleep since his wife had passed. His body ached a bit from sleeping on the couch, but his head felt clear and light. He sat up and cracked his neck, rolled over and cut a fart before standing up and moving toward the kitchen to prepare some coffee. The pot dripped slowly, and Robert watched the dark liquid begin to puddle up in the pot. He glanced at Hank, who watched the old man closely. They walked toward the door to relieve themselves outside. Robert unzipped his pants and began swaying in the morning air, pissing on the forest floor as Hank targeted a nearby tree to do the same.

The coffee tasted good. Robert finished his first cup quickly and poured a second. He glanced down at the coffee table, where he saw some of his paperwork. He knew he needed to review the contracts, bank loans and other work-related things. This morning would be a good time, no distractions, but he had to leave and let himself into Ray's Place before it opened a couple hours from now.

Robert would often let himself into the bar before Ray got there in the morning. He was the only guy with a key outside Ray's immediate family. Often, Robert would hide out there in the mornings when he was not out in the field - the dark confines helped relax him. Robert tied his boots, grabbed his paperwork and headed for his truck. Hank followed with curiosity and Robert smiled as the dog jumped into the cab. Robert started the truck and walked back toward the house to grab one last cup of coffee for the road. Hank sat in the driver's seat waiting for Robert to return.

The old man returned a few minutes later with a smile and a bone for Hank. The dog wagged his tail in a vigorous fashion, eagerly grabbing the bone and darting across the cab. Robert coughed and laughed as he lit a smoke and turned the truck around, heading for the tavern.

The parking lot was empty, as it was most of the time early Sunday morning. Sometimes a few rigs would still be parked in the lot after a weekend night, but this morning it was abandoned. Robert quickly headed for the back door. He walked in and the stale smoke of cigarettes and beer hit him harder than it normally did, causing him to mumble, "Fuck, Ray, you ever clean this place?" Hank followed Robert inside and laid down against the wall, chewing his bone, eyes fixated on Robert's every move. The old man dropped his paperwork on the large table against the back wall and walked around the bar to start the grill and coffee pot. While waiting, he poured himself a tall glass of beer and walked back to his work.

Robert began addressing some of the paperwork as he sipped his morning brew. A few minutes after eight, Ray walked through the already opened back door to greet Robert. "How goes it?"

"Good, 'n you?"

Ray set down some things on the bar and glanced at the grill and coffee pot. "Not bad. Missed you and Billy in here last night."

Robert set the empty glass down on the bar. "Yeah, Billy and Annie went to the coast yesterday, and I, well, I just fell asleep on the couch."

"Hell, it's been too long since I went to the coast," Robert agreed, as he opened the fridge and grabbed the bacon and eggs.

"I can get that, Robert. Get back to your work," Ray said as he poured himself a cup of coffee.

"Nah, shit Ray, sit down and relax while you can."

Ray shook his head. "Go sit down, for Christ sakes. I've seen you cook and it ain't pretty."

Robert chuckled in response, grabbed a cup of coffee and returned to his seat. Ray turned on the television for background noise and began frying up some food.

Sunday mornings were usually slow, as most of the folks were either going to church or recovering from a late night, and some were doing both. It was a peaceful time in the tavern, and both Ray and Robert liked it that way. Being the only show in town, Ray was doing fine for business, at least for now, and when these mornings were slow, he took advantage of them by cooking and watching television. As the hours passed, a few regulars showed up, usually just for a quick drink or two in between running errands.

Hank began to get restless, and Robert let him out and eventually put the dog in his truck, along with the paperwork. Returning to the bar, he took his seat and watched some television while he and Ray continued their conversation about work and life. Every time he ripped into the paperwork, it caused him stress. Things were getting more expensive, pay was going up, and too many folks relied on him to get things done. He shook his head and sipped his beer.

35

Billy awoke just before Annie and heard Chris in the other room talking to himself as he tossed things around. Billy chuckled as Annie moved around a little in his arms. Minutes later, the front door slammed and a truck started. Billy glanced outside to watch his friend leave for work. He rested his head on the pillow and kissed Annie's forehead. She lifted her head and gave Billy a soft kiss. Billy smiled and began messaging her leg. She resisted initially, but then rolled over and gave Billy her back. He rolled over beside her and began rubbing her hips and legs. She nestled closer, welcoming his touch. They rocked back and forth, him holding her hips she lifted her exposed arm and placed her hand behind his neck. He began to caress his hand along her stomach and breasts as they whispered to one another.

"You feel good," she said as she pressed her head against the pillow.

Billy paused in response, "You do, too." They continued on, eventually stopping and resting with each other. Billy separated himself and sat up, rolled off the bed and headed to the bathroom. Annie watched as he walked away naked. She smiled and closed her eyes again as she arched her back. Billy returned moments later.

"Let's get up; I'm fucking hungry."

"Give me a minute."

Billy shook his head at her and began getting dressed. He sat down in a nearby chair and watched as Annie struggled to get up. She finally gave Billy an impatient smile and lifted herself up.

"You look good," Billy said with a smile, lighting a smoke. Annie squinted and yawned, pushing away the hair in her face. The sheets dropped below her, exposing her breasts to the morning's cool air. Billy smiled and watched. Annie noticed and covered herself up.

The two sat silent, staring at each other, both trying to read into each other's thoughts. Billy walked toward the window to look outside. The sun was shining; the morning winds were pushing the seagulls throughout the beach that sat just a few blocks away. In the distance, he could see a few fishing boats leaving the bay towards the sea, bouncing as they met the waves and wind.

Annie began dressing, moving slowly. "I need some coffee," she said as she put her pants on, slapping her stomach as she paused to admire it. Billy returned his attention to Annie.

"Yeah, I could go for a few cups." Billy went to look around the house as Annie remade the bed. She found Billy outside watching the birds overhead. They walked toward the old part of town, where they entered a yuppie breakfast place. Annie was excited at the menu and the chance to hear the older folksinger who entertained the early risers.

They ate and listened to the man sing about local issues and hard times. Billy finished his food fast, sat back and drank several cups of coffee. Annie took her time, admiring the art and decorations that lined the ceilings and walls, occasionally shaking her head in appreciation to the rhythm of the guitar. Her food was delicious and she scraped the remaining bits with her leftover toast. Billy was surprised as he watched Annie. He stretched his back and went to pay the bill. Annie turned her attention to the singer, as he finished his last song of the morning. She had hoped for more songs, but she realized Billy was eager to get going, as he gave Annie the universal nod and headed for the door. She grabbed her things.

Outside, more locals and tourists were lining the streets, admiring the shops and running errands. The fog bank was rolling in earlier than expected, the sky a collision of sunshine to the east and grayness to the west.

They eventually found the truck where they had left it the night before, and began the slow trip back home. "You want to take the same way back?" Billy asked with a smile.

She looked at him and said with an obnoxious tone, "Yeah, that would be great." She leaned back in the seat and set her hands on her stomach, face leaning toward the passenger window. The truck had left the city limits and was eastbound, leaving the coastal winds and hitting the summer heat. Silence overcame the two and both welcomed it. Billy lost himself with the passing cars and trucks along the winding road. Annie's thoughts raced in several different directions leading to various question and answers of their future uncertainty.

Billy broke the silence and glanced toward her. "Are you scared?"

Annie paused and looked at Billy. "A little bit. I mean, I did not expect this to happen, but looking back on it, I guess I was a little careless, and maybe that is what I wanted."

Billy nodded. The reality was still new and confusing. Instead of addressing the issue, he often distracted himself from it, something he had learned from his father. She gazed back toward the passing homes and forested hillsides that came and went. The lush green understory was beginning to cure itself out due to the unusually dry summer.

"What should we name him?" Billy asked with a smile.

"What makes you think it's going to be a boy?" Annie asked with a concerned look.

"He is a McDonough; we always have boys."

"How do you know? There is no way to tell that."

"I just do. It's a boy."

"Well, I think it's a girl. There are more girls in my family than there are boys," she said, folding her arms and waiting for a response from Billy.

"Think what you may, but that's a boy inside of you, sure as shit."

Annie shook her head, fully aware that there was no way to tell, but not willing to childishly continue the conversation. She paused and changed the subject slightly. "Are you willing to have this baby?"

Billy looked at her for a second, then returned his eyes to the road. "Well, I don't have much choice in that, do I?"

Annie nodded in agreement. "Are you willing to change for the kid?"

Billy paused at the question and bit his lip. "What do you mean by that?"

Annie looked outside. "The drinking and things."

Billy turned the truck to pass a slower motorhome in the way. He did not respond immediately, as his attention was turned to passing the slower vehicle. "I mean, I guess, yeah. I won't be hanging out at Ray's every night while you're home with the kid, if that's what you mean."

"Are we going to get our own place?" Annie asked, trying to pry out as much information as possible, forcing Billy to make decisions and think about things other than logging and drinking.

"Yeah, thought we already talked about it."

Annie nodded. "Okay, when do you want to look for a place?"

Billy darted a look over to her and then back to the highway. "Fuck, I don't care, whenever."

"I just don't know if we should live in Hemlock or head into the valley where there are more things happening."

"What do you mean, Annie?"

"Well, I plan on working too, Billy, and it's not going to be waiting tables in Hemlock."

Billy arched his back and reached for a smoke. He had trouble lighting it as the truck wove its way around a curvy section in the highway. He did not respond, instead taking a long drag of smoke and exhaling slowly.

"Does that bother you?" Annie asked, arms still folded, searching for answers.

"Does what bother me?"

"That I don't want to live in Hemlock?"

"Not really. I mean, if there is work in Hemlock, I'll probably be in Hemlock though, and now ain't the time to bail on my dad."

"Isn't the mill closing down anyway?" Annie asked, disgusted at his response.

"Look, this is where I am at right now, 'n my dad ain't got much to lean on, 'n I ain't gonna bail on him tomorrow 'cause we got a kid on the way."

"I just want to give the kid something else besides this town!"

"Don't you think we are jumping ahead a little fast?" he asked, driving the truck fast into a gravel shoulder and slamming on the brakes, causing Annie to place both hands on the dashboard.

"Look, we just found out yesterday about this. Can we take our time and figure this out later?" he said, rolling down his window to spit outside. She watched and her eyes began to tear up.

"I just wanted you to know how I feel." She placed her hands on top of her eyes and shook her head.

"I already know how you feel," Billy said as he sat back in the truck and pulled the emergency break, letting his foot off the clutch and setting its gear to neutral.

"I'm sorry, I just want you to want more, and I want us to want more than just what we have now," she said, sobbing, shaking her head, and lifting her red eyes toward his. He shook his head. "I should not have brought this up now. I mean, it's not important today, but it will be in the weeks and months ahead. I am just confused, and I think I am scared and have no one else to talk to; no one else I love but you."

Billy rubbed his face and neck in response, lightly tapping the steering wheel.

"Listen, I know you're uncertain about a lot of things. Jesus, so am I, but think of me, too. I mean, shit, you were in Seattle just a few months back, 'n I had a mom and a brother just half a year ago. My life is fucked up right now and I am trying my best to keep my dad from killing himself, you know? I ain't as smart as you. Can't just pack up and go and be successful somewhere else."

He paused, looking off into the hillsides. "This is my home, the woods, the hills; that's what I know; that's what I am good at; that's what I love."

Annie began to cry harder and tears began to roll down her cheeks. Her nose began to run.

"I ain't saying that I won't leave, but now ain't the time to beg and plead. Hell, we ain't even married yet?"

She lifted her head and gazed at him, his eyes wide open and alert, poised and awake. "Should we get married?" she asked.

Billy glanced at her quickly and then threw the truck in gear and began to drive back onto the road. "Probably!"

The two sat silent, ignoring each other. The roads eventually led them to the city limits of Hemlock, where Billy pulled up to Annie's mom's house. He parked the truck and lifted his arm around Annie. "Why don't you go see your mom and talk with her, and I'll see you later tonight."

Annie shrugged at the idea, but realized Billy needed some room. "Okay, but hurry. My mom drives me nuts," she said, laughing as she wiped her tears.

Billy smiled and gave her a kiss on her forehead. "I will, and try to enjoy your time with her." Annie shut the door. Billy watched momentarily, then skidded out as he pulled away from the driveway.

36

"Hello, Mom," Annie said as she shut the door behind her. The house smelled of rotten food and stale cigarette smoke. Her mother was not much of a housekeeper, as the few dishes that Annie had noticed last time in the sink still remained. She shook her head in disapproval as she walked toward the living room where her mom was sitting.

"Why are you crying, dear?" her mother asked, finishing her glass of scotch.

"I'm pregnant," Annie replied, leaning back against the couch, folding her arms and glancing at the television.

"Oh, Jesus," her mother said as she got up for a refill.

"Thanks, Mom, for your love and support."

"Is it Billy's kid?"

Annie shook her head at the question as she watched her mother enter the kitchen and raised her voice. "Yes, it is."

"Well, he is a good kid, strong, good family," she muttered as she glanced at Annie and took another sip of her drink on her return to her chair in the living room. Annie raised her eyebrows at the comment and waited to see if her mother had anything else to say. Instead, her mother waited for Annie to say something, content with her seat and drink.

"I just don't know what I want, but it's not here. I don't want to wait for Billy every day to come back from the woods, knowing that every morning he leaves may be the last."

Her mother sat back and gently rocked in the chair. "This ain't the city life you know so well. Just be patient and take your time with things here. He may come around, but don't rush it. Don't push him away when you need him most."

Annie leaned forward and listened, and for once, her mother's comments struck a chord and made sense, made her think and silence her usual quick reaction of frustration. She ignored the annoyance of her mother's drinking and lack of appreciation for anything. Annie welcomed the silence and watched the daytime television with the older woman, who got lost in crossword puzzles and the background noise.

Her thoughts drifted toward Billy as her eyes closed and relaxed. She lifted her feet up, grabbed the blanket on the couch, and lost herself deep in dreams. Dreaming of times ahead, their kid running around the yard, in some other town, free from the loud and drunken roars from the tavern or big trucks racing down the streets, free from the smells of saw fuel and diesel, free from the saw chips on hickory shirts, or the mud and sweat on socks and boots. Billy looked different, not like he did now, thinner and cleaner, and he spoke differently. Annie almost did not recognize him. Their child was dirty after playing in the yard and chasing their dog, a Lab, golden in color, its coat shining in the midday sun. Their garden appeared bright with flowers and vegetables, creating colorful shades against their white house in the near distance. She knelt in the garden picking tomatoes, yelling at Billy to help her out. He hesitated and eventually walked toward her, his face different than before, almost unrecognizable. He spoke much differently than she expected, in a tone with a foreign accent. She sat puzzled, looking up at him, squinting as the sun blocked her view, unable to see his eyes. His head eventually blocked the sun and she saw another man standing there with a welcoming smile and hand.

Gasping for air, she lifted her head. The television was still on, her mother still sitting there. "You were dreaming of something," her mother said as she lit a cigarette. Annie sat up with a perplexed face. "Do you remember what about?" her mother asked as she put down the crossword puzzle.

Annie did not want to replay the memory in her mind. "No, I don't."

She got up, folded the blanket and placed it back on the couch. She walked toward the kitchen and glanced at the dirty dishes. The sun was hot outside and a few flies had entered the kitchen, preying on the leftover crumbs and filth that had been awaiting their presence. Annie swatted at a few and killed a couple as she began washing some of the dirty dishes. Her mother noticed her attempts and quickly stated, "You don't have to do that. I will get around to them eventually."

Shaking her head and biting her lip, she responded, "That's all right, Ma. I will just get them out of the way." Her mother mumbled something that she could not hear over the running water. Within minutes, she had finished the dishes and said her goodbyes. She opened the door and welcomed the afternoon sunshine.

37

Billy had not wasted any time after dropping off Annie. He pointed his truck toward the tavern to see his father. He wore a big smile as he parked the truck and opened the front door of the bar.

"Line 'em up, Ray!" he shouted across the bar as he walked up to his father, who responded with a half-drunken look. "I'm going to be a father!"

From the dozen or so folks in the bar, loud screams and yells followed, as Ray tried his best to find enough shot glasses. Lee came over and gave Billy a slap on the back, then retreated to the other side of the bar to help Ray serve drinks.

Robert smiled with surprise, but waited for the excitement to subside before addressing his son, who was inundated with various slaps and yells as folks drank their drinks in celebration. After a few shots and several congratulatory remarks later, folks began to give the father and son a chance to talk. The two sat silently, unable to address each other, smiling at others and ignoring their own need to talk. Billy gave his father room as Ray and he talked about other things. Robert sat still, biting his lip in surprise and joy. He did not know how to show affection or praise. He wanted to throw his arms around his son, but couldn't do it, not here, not in front of everyone. Billy knew this and watched as tears appeared in his father's eyes.

Ray left to serve their friends further down the bar. Robert looked his son over. "I have never been prouder of you, boy. You'll make a good father."

"Thanks, Pops," Billy said, smiling at his dad, who bit his tongue, trying to hold back any obvious emotions.

"You know, I dropped off Annie at her mom's house and I was driving down the street and it hit me like a ton of bricks. I want to be with this girl; she's a good one."

Robert nodded in approval. "Life ain't worth living if you can't share it with a woman, Billy." Taking a long sip of beer, Robert looked his son over, smiled, lifted his arm up, grabbed his son's neck and rocked him back and forth. Billy's eyes began to fill and a lump grew in his throat. He ignored it the best he could, as did his father, who stared at his feet and tried to run away from his tears.

"Here's to you, Billy, you fucking little bastard!" shouted Lee from across the bar, causing the two McDonoughs to separate and smile. Everyone lifted their drinks and yelled in support.

Annie smiled as she heard the yelling from outside. She had enjoyed her walk through the town and had expected Billy to let everyone know their news. As she opened the door, everyone screamed with support. The other ladies in the bar came up to her with welcoming hugs. "Congrats, Annie!" Lee shouted from across the bar. Annie smiled back at him. She welcomed Billy's hug as he brought her close.

Robert glanced at her with a smile. "I just heard the news. That's good to hear. Proud to be your new father."

Annie smiled back. "Well, thank you, Dad." Laughing, she brushed back a few tears. Billy smiled at the two as he sipped his beer. The three began to talk about their trip to the coast. An hour came and went as the two men drank their beers with plenty of laughs. Annie sat patiently, enjoying much of the half-drunken talk. Billy picked up on it and before long offered a retreat, which she accepted. Stopping by the store, they picked up some supplies for dinner and drove home. Another day of work awaited, another week where Annie tried to stay busy, now nursing a new avenue of life.

38

The morning came quickly for Billy, who struggled to leave the warm confines of the bed with Annie, who kissed his neck as he squinted and stretched himself awake. Nothing was coming easy for Billy that morning. He tripped over his boots and landed on Annie, who griped in pain. "Sorry, honey," he said.

Rolling over to watch Billy dress, she said, "That's okay. Have a good day, okay?" Billy nodded as he carried his boots to the next room and began packing a lunch.

Red was waiting for Billy outside his house as he normally did. Throwing his gear into the back of the truck, he entered the cab and took a dip of chew. "Where's Hank?"

Billy grabbed the can of chew. "He's hanging out with Annie. Didn't want to come and work."

Red shook his head. "Can't find good help anymore."

Laughing, Billy took a large dip and pointed the truck toward the work site.

Winding up and down the roads, Billy finally broke the news. "Annie's pregnant."

Red looked at Billy with a smile. "Is it yours?"

Billy, laughing in response, rolled down his window to spit. The truck rolled to a stop as he gazed across the canyon down toward the town of Cadillac. "Yeah, she says it is." He parked the truck and laughed as he got out and took a piss. Red glanced down the canyon towards the mill. They could not see many logs remaining in the yard near the mill. It was several miles away, but it had been several weeks since any of their loads had gone there. The mill officials said they had some mechanical problems, but everyone knew this was not the case.

Red exited the truck and glanced down the ridge. "You think they are done?" he asked Billy, who stood watching the scenery.

"I don't fucking know, man. You've been around a lot longer than I have, but I would say yes, just waiting around to hear yes, you know?"

Red nodded, "Yeah, it's a done deal, no question in my mind, man; matter of days or weeks." Billy gave Red a concerned look. Red looked back and continued, "I have seen this shit go back and forth for years, but now it almost has to happen. If the company ain't investing anything anymore and they have been talking about it for this long, it's gonna happen. Plus, they are running out of timber, too."

Billy kicked the dirt below his boots and continued to look down the ridge at the distant homes near the mill with portions of the nearby lake exposed. Red squinted and spit out his chew, clearing his throat. "You know, many years ago I got a woman pregnant and she wanted me to quit." He paused and looked at Billy, who looked back at him. "But I was fucking stubborn and ignored it. She ended up leaving for somewheres."

Billy stood up straight and spit out his chew. "So you got a kid out there somewhere, eh?" Red nodded.

"The shitty part about all that is that I ended up coming out here not long after she left. I yelled and screamed that I would never leave, and then I did about a year later." Red paused. "No one knows that about me."

"I'll keep it that way," Billy said.

Both men retreated back to the truck to continue on to the work site. Silence followed for a while as they drove along the two-track road. Red eventually interrupted it. "You going to run off with Annie?"

Billy looked quickly at Red. "Why you think I'm going to leave?"

Red lifted his eyebrows. "That woman ain't the kind to hang out and wait for you to do the things we do." Billy ignored the comment and continued to drive. "Hey, it might be a good thing. You really want to do this for another 30 years - that is, if you don't get killed before then?"

"Shit, Red, I like the work. You know that."

"Yeah, but I was in love once, and it changes you, makes you do things that you would not normally do, makes you think things you wouldn't normally think. Man, the power of the pussy can fuck with your mind."

Billy laughed, but he nodded in agreement. "I got no intentions on leaving. Plus if I go, then you would actually have to produce something."

Red laughed. "I lay more wood down in an hour than you do in a day," Red said.

"Red, where is your fucking walker?" The two started laughing as they approached the landing where the equipment was staged.

Minutes later, the rest of the crew showed up. Billy gave a quick briefing, but before he could escape to his truck, Red gave an announcement of Billy's news. Billy leaned against his truck, smiling and shaking his head as the crew harassed him for several minutes. Red eventually walked over and slapped his shoulder. "You didn't think you were going to get away with it, did you?"

Billy laughed and stood up. "Nah, just hoped to, that's all."

39

Robert was still celebrating Monday at the tavern. He had stopped back down there after running a few errands and met up with Lee and Ray for some cards. From time to time, when the mornings and afternoons were slow and they could avoid work, the three would argue and gamble for hours. Oftentimes they would end up teaming up against the odd man out and would tell embarrassing stories over and over again. It never got old, at least not to them.

"Damn it, Robert, you took all my money again," Lee shouted as he sat up and walked towards the bathroom, shaking his head with disgust.

"You boys need to buy some poker faces. Hell, I haven't had a good hand all day," Robert yelled, laughing in between coughs. He stood up to stretch his back and walked around the bar. "I guess I'll buy the next round," he said, smirking at Ray, who shook his head in frustration at losing.

As Ray returned to the bar to begin prepping for the afternoon rush, the door opened and five well-dressed strangers walked in, the last one locking the front door as he followed the rest of his friends. Robert stopped dead in his tracks and sized them up, lit a smoke and exhaled. "You fellas lost?"

The oldest of the five smiled at Robert before nodding to one of the men, who walked toward Robert. Lee interrupted the encounter. "You guys want something to drink?"

The older stranger stared at Ray for a second, then looked around the empty bar. "Yeah, whiskey for everyone." Ray nodded and raised his eyebrows at Robert, whose humor had been replaced by concern. Lee had finished up in the bathroom and strutted toward Robert, gazing as the pack leaned against the bar just a few feet away. Lee, half drunk, without a care in the world, spoke up.

"The hairdresser is down the street a few blocks." This caused a few laughs among the small crowd. The old man stood motionless, stone-faced, eyeing Robert.

"Robert, you want to hear what I have to say," the older gentleman said as he inhaled his smoke.

"I could care less what you think or say. Hell, I wouldn't cross the street to piss on you if you were on fire," Robert said, throwing his smoke down and scraping his boot against the wood floor to put it out.

"Cadillac is done. Town's dead; mill's gone. Gonna burn the fucker to the ground," the old man said as he welcomed the whiskey and raised it to his friends and enemies.

"Shut the fuck up," Lee said as Robert bit his tongue and glanced at the clock. If he could hold these guys here for another half hour or so, his crew would be showing up. At least these bastards would get a beat down. But now, they were outmanned and outgunned. Robert turned to Lee and told him to sit down. Lee hesitated but listened. The older man watched as Robert took a few steps forward.

"Why the fuck are you here?"

The older man laughed and gestured for another drink. "Trust me, I don't want to be here, but I was told to ask you to consider your bit of land before we burn the fucking town down."

"Why would you burn Cadillac?" Ray asked.

One of the men interrupted his question. "How about you fix us up another round and mind your own business."

Robert pointed his finger at the younger kid. "How about you shut the fuck up and let the man talk." The boy smiled, clenching his fist.

The old man set down his drink, staring at the mirror behind the bar that showed the entire room. "I was warned about you, that you were an old, crotchety bastard, and you are. Now I know why your wife died on you. Hell, I would have prayed for cancer, too."

Robert stood up and walked toward the old man, but the younger kid stepped in his way and went to grab Robert, who evaded the attempt and slammed his forehead into the kid's nose, breaking the cartilage and sending blood rushing down his suit. Another youthful visitor rushed Robert, but was met with a beer glass across the face. Lee moved in closer as Robert jumped on the wounded kid, punching him in the face in a rapid fashion. The older man rotated in his bar stool as the two other visitors reached for their handguns and strutted toward Robert and Lee. Robert continued to punch the kid, blood gushing with each punch. One man placed a kick in Robert's ribs that sent him rolling off the boy. Robert started to get up, but was hit with a gun across the back of the head, sending him to the ground. The other man cocked his revolver at Lee, who raised his hands and stepped back.

Ray stood motionless. His guns were in the back room and there was not much he could do with two guns pointed at his friends. Robert rose up on all fours, coughing as he tried to catch his breath. His two victims rolled over, got up and walked away, trying to nurse their wounds. The young kid's nose was still spitting blood, his nose twisted in the wrong direction.

After several more kicks, Robert eventually could not get up and rolled over, grabbing his stomach in pain, his face now bloody from a few blows. The old man got up from the barstool and stood over Robert. "Do we look like amateurs to you?"

One of Robert's eyes was closing on him and his nose dripped blood. He coughed and spit some blood out on the floor. "You look like a bunch of faggots."

The old man chuckled as he lit another smoke and gestured to one of the men with a gun, who kicked Robert again in the ribs, causing Robert to scream in frustration. Robert watched as the old man walked away and handed the kid his handkerchief.

"What did you think was going to happen, Robert; that you could just bully a few folks around and they would do what you wanted? We are just too big of an outfit to put up with you. Your business is irrelevant to us. You are a dime a dozen. No loss. Crews are the same. You cut and haul; big fucking deal." The old man gestured to his crew as he walked toward the door.

The old man turned one last time to look at the three men watching as they walked away. Robert spit more blood and tried to stand up, using the bar as a guide. The crew watched. "Go fuck yourself," Robert said as he stood up, smiling, blood filling his mouth and covering teeth as he grinned.

The old man smiled as he put his sunglasses on and left the tavern. Lee rushed to the window and watched as they hoped in two identical black Mercedes. Ray rushed across the bar to help Robert sit down at a nearby booth.

40

Annie had come to town to check out some books at the public library and when she pulled onto Main Street, she saw the two black sedans rush east through town. She paused and watched, pondering why they were here, then figured they were lost. It was odd to see that type of car in the area, something she had not seen for awhile. Heading back toward the house, she spotted the sheriff running code behind her as she pulled over to let him pass. Curious, she slowly followed as the sheriff skidded to a stop in Ray's parking lot. Annie made her way there a few minutes later and walked in to see what was happening.

Robert was sitting with a towel across his head and his ribs wrapped in ice. Annie rushed over to find out what happened. The sheriff was sitting on a bar stool shaking his head in frustration. "You want me to go pull them fuckers over, Robert?"

Annie lifted her head toward the sheriff in approval, but Robert shot back, "Nah, fuck them. Don't waste your time." She began to assess the injuries and recommended that Robert be taken to the hospital in Dallas, but he refused and gestured for a drink.

She could feel her pulse race, wondering where Billy was, scared at his reaction, concerned for Robert's condition. "What happened, Robert?" Annie asked as she studied his face.

Robert turned and grimaced in pain. Lee spoke for him. "Those damn sonsofbitches from the logging company came down here making threats 'n such. Robert got kicked a few times after he called them a bunch of queers." Robert chuckled at Lee's assessment. Annie shook her head, too concerned to laugh.

Annie stood up and paced around the bar a little, shocked at what had happened, glancing at the men who sat near her. Robert sat back, sipped his beer and gave the sheriff a nod. He got up and walked toward the door. Annie followed the sheriff outside. "You're not going to do anything?"

The man turned toward her. "Robert don't want to press charges, and there ain't much I can do, ma'am." Annie shook her head and watched as he entered his cruiser.

She stood in the afternoon sun for a few seconds, squinting as she watched the cruiser disappear down a back street. Returning to the bar, she heard the old man complaining about the guys coming into the bar and demanding things. Robert gave Annie a fierce glare. Both were wondering when Billy would show, he and the crew, and what would happen when they saw Robert.

41

Billy and Red were silent on the way back to town. The shift had gone quickly, and after several conversations that day, they usually kept quiet on the trip back home. They pulled into Ray's parking lot just ahead of a few other rigs from the crew, then encountered a few more cars. The sheriff's rig had returned and was parked out front. A few folks stood outside talking. Red and Billy took notice of the peculiar situation, but neither said much.

One of the kids out front quickly got out of the entrance as Billy pushed the door open. He stopped momentarily when he saw his father across the bar, hunched over and bloody. Red shook his head as he followed Billy across the bar. "What the hell happened, Pops?" Billy asked as he looked at his dad, quickly turning to Ray and Lee. Robert lifted his head and shook it with disgust, embarrassed that he looked the way he did.

Ray responded, "Those fuckers from Columbia came in here barking nonsense and making threats."

Lee nodded. "They just left a few minutes ago, driving black Benzes heading east."

Billy took one last look at his father. He was banged up, but he knew he was all right; nothing his dad couldn't bounce back from in a bit. He got up, then noticed Annie sitting quietly in the booth nearby. He began pacing back and forth, trying to ignore the small talk going on around the bar. Billy walked toward the back deck as Annie followed. "Can't let them fuckers get away with this," he mumbled as he looked into Annie's concerned eyes.

She nodded, not trying to persuade him just yet. Annie threw her arms around him and tried to bring him close. He responded and hugged her back, but his mind was elsewhere.

"Are you okay?" he asked as he separated himself from her grip.

"I'm fine, Billy. Please just don't do anything stupid."

He smiled in response. "Listen, just go take care of dad and I'll be back in a few minutes." He left her on the deck and headed toward the back door to the tavern.

She cupped her mouth with her hands and shouted, "I love you." Billy turned as he entered the tavern and gave her a nod.

He glanced at Ray. "Go get your guns." Ray looked at Robert, who sat motionless. The sheriff lowered his head, not willing to get in the way. Red followed Billy, who grabbed the choker boys and headed out of the bar toward the parking lot with a few guns. They circled for a second. Billy grabbed the .45 and stuck it in his pants, then handed the shotgun to one of the choker boys, while the other grabbed one of the hunting rifles that Ray had. Red loaded a 30.06 as he waited to hear Billy's briefing. "Let's see if we can scare these fuckers. Follow my lead. Don't know where they're at, so it may be a wild goose chase." No one said anything as they jumped into two rigs; the boys in one, and Red and Billy in the other.

Billy lit a cigarette as he skidded the truck out of the parking lot and headed east. Red checked the rifle over, made sure it was loaded, and placed it between his legs. Billy sat stone-faced, cigarette dangling from his lips, speeding through town. Red watched as the signs and houses sped past faster than usual. "What's the plan, Billy?" The truck entered a curve and grazed the gravel on the side of the pavement, sending the back tire whipping a few feet. Red clenched the dashboard.

"Don't know yet, Red." The choker boys were a few hundred yards behind them, but keeping pace.

Just a few minutes from the city limits of Dallas, they began to see more homes on the hillsides and side streets. The first bar came into sight, but Billy was focused on the road. Red interrupted his thoughts. "There, black Benzes."

Adjusting quickly, Billy set his foot on the brakes and entered the turn fast, skidding the tires. Two men stood by the cars, nursing their wounds and smoking cigarettes. In a matter of a few seconds, Billy slid the truck into one of the parked cars. "Take the back door, Red!" Billy shouted as he jumped from the truck, gun in hand. The choker boys slid past Billy and had guns aimed at the two men before they knew what hit them.

The two men stood speechless in surprise. The boys aimed silently, waiting for Billy's lead, waiting for one of the wounded men to make a move, poised and willing. Billy pointed at the ground as he headed for the main door. One of the boys walked toward Billy; the other signaled the men to rest on their knees, hands on their heads.

Billy kicked in the door and quickly glanced down the bar. The old man sat alone, sipping a drink and reading a newspaper while his two friends were shooting pool. Billy walked behind the man preparing to shoot his ball. He grabbed the pool stick and swung at the man's head, breaking the stick, sending it flying against the wall. The other man jumped at Billy, but was too late, as Billy sent his forehead into the man's nose, crushing it, blood spilling down his shirt. The man threw his cupped hands over his nose as he fell to the table, dripping blood onto the green felt.

The old man leaned forward, searching for his gun in his resting sports coat, but was too late. Billy had his gun pointed at the man's head with a smile. Red appeared from the back room, rifle pointed at the men, scanning the room for targets. Red stopped just a few feet away and aimed at the one man, who reached for his gun and pointed it at Billy. He grimaced in pain as his head throbbed from the pool stick, hand swaying as he pointed.

"You must be the avenging son?" the old man said as he sat up and reached for his scotch. Billy's eyes were wide open as he strutted toward the man, gun pointed at him. The front door opened as the choker boys led the remaining men inside. The old man looked around the room and was surprised. He gestured to the one remaining armed friend and advised him to lower his gun. The choker boy walked over and grabbed it from him with a smile.

The bartender stood frozen, hands on the bar, watching as the tension grew. "The guy tending bar might call the cops, so you may want to run along," the old man said as he took a drag from his cigarette.

Billy lifted his eyes from the old man and looked at the bartender with a grin. "Doubt it. I used to play football against him." The bartender smirked, somewhat concerned.

Billy returned his eyes to the old man. "Did you think you were going to die today?"

The old man fiddled with his mustache and smiled. "No son, I didn't, especially not by a young little redneck fucker like yourself."

Billy nodded. "You must have some really big balls."

Smiling, the older man responded, "It ain't the first time I have had a gun pointed at me."

The crowd stood speechless listening to the two men exchange words. The older man continued, "I should have finished your father off back at the bar. That stubborn son of a bitch does not know how to listen."

Billy lowered his gun, walked toward one of the boys and traded his handgun for the shotgun. The older man had a concerned look as he watched Billy return. He paused and released the side-by-side barrel to confirm it was loaded, and snapped it back into place. Billy stood above the old man, who smirked at him and raised his glass to take a sip. Billy smiled back as he shoved the shotgun into the glass, sending the glass and barrel into the man's mouth. Glass shattered across the man's face as the barrel broke through his teeth. The man's eyes began to water as his arms flopped around in pain. Billy kicked the man's chair out from under him, sending him to the floor, begging with the shotgun still stuck in his mouth, blood now running down his chin along with shattered glass and teeth.

"I believe you were saying something?" Billy asked with a smile. The man cupped his hands together in a praying manner, pleading for Billy to stop, but Billy stood his ground, smiling in a sinful way. Red squinted in disgust as he scanned the room to witness the concerned faces, watching to see what Billy would do next.

He could see the fear in the man's eyes, but Billy would not back off, not yet, not until they knew not to fuck with him or his father again. Billy kept one hand on the gun as he looked at everyone in the room, one by one, and watched their faces. Many of the men looked to the ground as Billy searched for their eyes. One of the choker boys nodded in approval, waiting for orders. Billy acknowledged the kid's dedication. He returned to the older man, now on his knees, gun still lodged in his mouth.

He took a step back and pulled the gun away, watching as blood, glass and teeth spilled to the floor. The old man dropped to the ground, rocking back and forth, crying in a fetal position. Billy knelt beside him and lifted the man's chin with his hand. "This is your only chance. I don't care if you close down the mill. I don't care what your company does, but if I see you around here again, I will fucking kill you. Every one of you fuckers here is dead the next time you set foot in this county." The men nodded, waiting to be released, ready to return to their homes far away from the hills and woods.

Billy stood up and spit on the floor, glancing back at the old man as he threw the gun on his shoulder. "You should know better than to mess with a man's family." The man nodded as he lay bleeding and in pain. Billy glanced at Red and walked toward the door. Red and the choker boys followed Billy outside. A thunderstorm was passing overhead and a brief stint of summer rain was hitting the gravel parking lot where they stood.

Billy looked at Red. "Why don't you ride back with the boys." Red said nothing as he followed the two boys toward their truck. Billy hopped in his truck and threw it in reverse, causing it to skid out and send rocks in various directions.

It took awhile before the choker boys left the parking lot, with a few minutes passing as they argued over seating positions and placed the guns behind the seat. Billy had sped off back toward Hemlock in a rush. Eventually, the boys got close enough to see Billy's taillights a mile ahead. Red encouraged the boys to drive faster as they left Dallas behind. Everyone was eager to get back to Hemlock.

Billy raced around every turn, listening as his tires whined with the recent moist streets. He wanted to get home quickly to see Annie and make sure his dad was truly all right. His forehead ached as he adjusted the rearview mirror to look at a slight bruise forming on his head. Billy returned his eyes back to the highway long enough to see an oncoming car drift into his lane. He swerved to avoid hitting the reckless car, causing the truck to fishtail across the highway. He tried to correct it, but he lost control of the truck as it shot off the road into a slight ravine, sending its front end into a large stump.

Billy's mind allowed him briefly to recall an image of himself as a child, fishing alongside his father at their creek, before his ribs crashed into the steering wheel, cracking them like twigs. His lungs gasped for air with one quick sigh as his head whipped back, lashing against the rearview window and causing it to crack. His body tumbled throughout the cab like clothes in a washing machine as the truck rolled over several times as it fell along the ravine. It finally stopped a couple hundred feet from the highway along some small trees.

His sight began to grow dim until it was if he had entered a dark room, desperately trying to find a light switch or something, but unable to do so. Annie's voice was there, though soft and unreadable. He tried, but could not understand her words. His mind began to wind down slowly, sinking without content. His eyes shut; darkness ensued.

42

The three men said little as they drove towards Hemlock, hanging on as the boy tested his tread with the wet road. Red stared out the window, surprised that his heart still thumped hard against his chest. They leaned into the last sharp curve before a long straightaway when Red thought he saw a truck lying down below the ledge. He looked ahead, expecting to see taillights, but did not. "Hold up, kid." The boy pulled over.

"What, Red?"

"Put it in reverse. A few hundred feet back, thought I saw something."

The kid sent the truck in reverse. They stopped at a point where they saw tracks leaving the road. Red jumped out of the truck. "Fuck, there is a truck down there." The two other boys followed Red as he jumped down the ravine, following the truck's path through the brush. Red got closer. "Oh, Jesus, oh, fuck. Billy!" Red slid down a few feet just short of the truck and looked up at one of the boys. "Go get some fucking help!" The boy nodded and ran up the hill without any hesitation.

Red reached through the broken glass and grabbed Billy's limp arm. He shouted at Billy, but heard no response. He lay flat down in the mud, trying to see if Billy was moving, but he was not. He grabbed Billy's shoulders and began pulling the kid out of the truck, placing his hand on his chest and feeling his broken ribs. Billy lay motionless.

Red noticed a little blood coming from his head, but saw a fair amount of bruising on the kid's head and chest. Billy's eyes were open, lost, staring into space. Red glared at them, praying for a response. Red sat back, Billy staring at him. He reached over and closed the boy's eyes. The choker boy sat a few yards above Red and Billy, sitting silent, shaking his head in disbelief.

Red dragged his hands through the moist dirt and grabbed the soil, picking it up and dropping it. He sat back and rested his head against the ground, staring up at the tail end of the thunderstorm. The breeze picked up and blew a few leaves against his face. He sat up briefly before rising to his feet. Exhaling, he looked at Billy's truck and all the gear that lay in the brush. He grabbed the two saws lying in the brush and began walking up the hill toward the road. The choker boy took one last look at Billy and followed.

43

The phone rang amid the curious restless crowd at Ray's Place. Annie watched Ray as he drifted behind the bar to answer the phone. He stood motionless, listening to the caller, and she could tell something bad had happened. Ray hung up the phone and lowered his head. Many folks had been watching and were wondering what was said. He turned to the crowd and paused, looked at Annie with a sad look, and said, "Billy's truck went off the road about two miles east of here."

Annie leaped up, eyes wide open with fear. Robert pushed himself away from the table and followed Annie toward her truck. She left the parking lot with Robert a few seconds before anyone else. She raced through town, ignoring the concerning townsfolk who shook their heads at her speed.

The rain had ceased, but the silence was louder and more deadly than any noise or threat. Robert's body went numb as he bit his lip and clenched his fist in anticipation. The choker boy's truck was just up ahead as Annie slid along the shoulder, eventually stopping. Robert jumped from the truck, ignoring all his injuries. He leaped down the ravine with Annie slip sliding behind. Robert skidded to a stop just a few feet away from Billy, who was lying still next to his truck. "Oh, Jesus, wake up, boy," Robert said, grabbing his son's battered head, rocking it back and forth. Annie was just a few feet away and collapsed to the ground, crying uncontrollably.

With Billy's head in his lap, Robert continued to rock back and forth. "Oh shit, oh shit, c'mon now, son, wake up." Annie watched as Robert tried to wake Billy, who lay motionless. She sat with her arms around her knees, her head lifting and falling in prayer. After a few minutes, she found herself crawling over to Robert and Billy. Robert let Billy's head gently rest against the ground as he pushed himself away. Annie lay down beside Billy and began to caress his hair. She lay lost in thought, unable to hear Robert cursing behind her, unable to hear the sirens and the conversations on the roadside.

She caught her breath, lifting herself up. She was having a hard time breathing. She caught Robert's eyes focused on her. The two stood up and collided with a hug, closing their eyes, leaving the sight for just a moment to feel some life. She pushed him away and turned her back toward Billy. The old man glanced at his boy and then began cursing and kicking the truck until his body could not take it anymore. He fell to the ground, crying in frustration and guilt. Annie began to slowly walk back toward her truck. Robert scratched his hair in rapid fashion as he lifted himself up and stood above his son. He knelt on one knee, threw Billy's arms around his neck and squatted to pick his boy up. He rocked back and forth, trying to gain some footing, unable to keep balance with his boy on his shoulder. He dropped back to one knee. Grinding his teeth, he picked himself up and began to hike his kid toward the road.

Annie never looked back until she reached her truck, ignoring all the concerned townsfolk who offered their sympathies and help. Robert emerged from the brush, carrying his son. The choker boys dove off the cliff to help, but Robert yelled at them to clear the way. He stepped slowly, one foot in front of the other, staggering with his boy on his back. The crowd stood speechless, then scattered as Robert walked his boy to the choker boys' truck. No one moved or whispered.

44

Billy McDonough was buried two days later in the old Hemlock cemetery. He was laid down next to his mother and brother, and 17 other McDonough relatives. The ceremony took place on a warm morning, where dozens upon dozens of Billy's close friends and townsfolk gathered and paid their respects.

Annie sat motionless, wearing a long black dress, her eyeliner smearing with the tears that continued to roll down her cheek. The past couple of days had been trying, with nowhere to go to gain any comfort. She fell asleep one night in Billy's bed, but awoke in fear and anxiety. She tried her mother's house, but her mother did not provide any comforting insight, nor did the hours she spent talking and crying with Susie. For much of the ceremony, Annie stared at her feet, ignoring the short sermon from the local priest, but admiring the array of flowers that surrounded the tombstone and gravesite. Glancing around the cemetery, she noticed its small size. It rested on a hill overlooking much of the town and valleys to the east. The McDonough graves sat facing the west without a view, blocked by trees, but that was more fitting for their sake.

Robbie stood up to say a few words. Annie lifted her head to listen. Robert rocked gently back and forth, sitting next to her. Robbie's soft tone helped relax Annie. "…few people ever enter our lives that have the effect that Billy did. He was an emotional tattoo, one that was forever worn and cared for." Robbie paused and cleared his throat. "I always enjoyed our conversations about work and women, his curiosities ran thick, guiding his spirit and interest. He was strong, not just in physical strength, but emotional strength, too. He cared for his friends, loved his family and worked hard, if for no other reason than his own pride."

Robert continued to rock, shaking his head in agreement, biting his lip, and trying not to break down. Annie rested her hand on his and did her best to shed a smile. Robert welcomed it and griped her hand with his. They continued to listen. "Billy made us all want to be better people, his spirit infectious, his kindness unsurpassed, his heart larger than most. But, in the end, with his smile and voice, his bold stance and strut, I will remember him as a true woodsmen."

Robbie grabbed his notes and nodded toward Robert, who welcomed his respect. Robert picked himself up and shook Robbie's hand as he approached. Annie lifted her head with a smile, causing Robbie to drop to one knee and give her a hug.

Robert sat back down as folks began to mingle and separate themselves from the tombstone. The old man continued to sit, ignoring the eyes of many of his friends and co-workers. His were fixated on his two boys' and his wife's tombstones that rested just a few feet away from him. He shook his head in silence, his head still heavy from an explosive drunk the night before, agonizing in pain, ravaging the house by himself. Annie took a deep breath and laid her hand along Hank's head, who lay still beside her. He was a little nervous the past couple of days in Billy's absence.

A few close friends went up to Robert and offered their support. Lee and Ray began talking, but Robert ignored most of their words. Instead, his eyes lifted a few hundred feet up the hill toward a man who leaned against an oak tree. Robert could not make out who it was, but for some reason found interest in the man standing away from everyone else. He had been there the whole time, not willing to come any closer than he did. Annie noticed the man too, but showed no curiosity.

The crowd had begun to dissipate with just a few stragglers remaining to help Annie and Robert down to their truck, but the two were content helping themselves. The flowers stood bright and scenic, resisting the morning breeze as it ran upslope. Annie placed one last flower on the tombstone as she welcomed Robert's arm for support and they walked down to their truck. As they started the engine, only a few other vehicles remained. Most of the crowd had returned to their day. Both watched as the stranger began to walk toward the gravesite.

"I wonder who that man is?" Robert asked as he lit a cigarette and turned the key to start the truck.

"Probably just an old friend from school, too shy to show his face," she said, rolling down her window and welcoming the wind.

"You are probably right, just would like to know, that's all."

45

"God damn it, Billy! All those times running from trees, working in the hills, and you end up driving off the road?" the stranger said as he stood above the tombstone. He unbuttoned his sports coat, allowing the breeze to blow it around, cooling him down. His dark sunglasses reflected the scripture of the McDonough tombstones. He was taken back when he began to read all the McDonough family names that were buried here, many of the men dead at a young age.

He shook his head. "Been too long since we last crossed paths. I wish things could have been different for us." Taking a step back, he looked down the hill across the green lawn of the cemetery. A few tall fir trees still stood, providing peculiar shadows. Oak and various fruit trees lined the outskirts of the lawn. Shaking his head, he welcomed the light breeze blowing against his face. Across the ridge, he noticed the steep wooded slopes and the distant valley views to the east. It had been many years since he had been in Hemlock, and he did not remember the town being this scenic or quiet. The solitude brought him some change, but fear as well.

The stranger returned to look at Billy's tombstone. "I guess this is where you belong now, right here next to Mom and Boone." He knelt, placed an agate on the tombstone and stood up. He glanced down the winding little access road to see the last of the vehicles leaving, with only his rental car remaining.

Taking a deep breath, he shook his head and began to walk slowly toward his car. The rental was new, but smelled fake, some new car spray scent that made the man cringe as he sat. Glancing up at the site one last time, he started the car and began to drive back through town.

46

Neither Robert nor Annie felt like socializing as they drove by the packed parking lot at Ray's Place and continued down the winding road back to the house. They drove silently, both staring out the window and watching the truck weave its way around the curves. The house looked abandoned and quiet. Hank did not budge as the truck came to a stop. He eventually got up and followed Annie as they entered the house. It felt emptier than it looked.

"Do you want some coffee?" Robert asked as he tossed the keys down on the coffee table and glanced at Annie.

Whispering, "Yeah, that sounds nice," she walked to the dinner table and took a seat, reaching down to take off her black heels and began rubbing her feet. He returned a few minutes later with two cups. They gave each other a concerned smile and then gazed out the windows as they waited for the coffee to cool. Hank got up and walked toward Annie for a rub. She smiled at him and began messaging his ears until he sat and then lay down against her feet.

Annie studied Robert's worn-down, weathered face, noticing lines more prominent than before, his eyes bloodshot. She whispered, "What are you going to do now?"

Taking a sip, he brought his eyes back toward hers. "What do you mean?"

"I don't know, with work, I guess."

"I suppose I will go back to work in the morning." He paused and sat back. "It ain't just what I want; I got too many men relying on me for work and pay."

Annie nodded in agreement. She nursed her cup, enjoying the taste, rubbing her feet against the retriever's coat.

The phone rang, but Robert did not want to get up to answer it, so Annie did. She nodded a few times and wrote down a number. Hanging up, she sat down and stared at the number, shaking her head in disbelief.

"Who the hell was that?" Robert asked as he turned his attention toward her.

"My mom. I guess the law firm in Dallas called and wanted to know if I was still interested in a job." Annie cupped her hand over her mouth and looked at Robert, shaking her head. Robert leaned back in his chair, raised his eyebrows and took a sip of coffee.

"Well, that's a good thing, ain't it?"

Annie nodded, beginning to cry again. "Yes, I think so. It's just, it's just…"

Robert nodded. "Look, it's good to hear something good today, you know?"

She walked back toward the table and sat, teary-eyed. He interrupted the silence. "Well, you going to call them bastards?"

Annie smiled in response. "Yeah, I suppose I should."

Robert nodded with approval as he took another swig of coffee, set down the cup and looked her over. She stared out the window again, shaking her head in shock.

"What are you going to name the baby boy?" Robert asked with a grin, causing Annie to sway from one emotion to another.

She set down the coffee cup and took a breath. Hesitating, she smiled. "How do you know it's a boy?" It was the first time she had really smiled in a few days.

"Because McDonoughs always have boys," Robert said, smiling.

"You know, Billy said the same damn thing," Annie said, shaking her head, causing her to laugh. Robert started laughing and coughing at the comment. He leaned over and grimaced, as his ribs still ached from the beating a few days ago.

"Well, I guess I did something right in raising him," he said, his smile changing to a look of concern.

Annie's smile turned more serious as she studied Robert's face. "You did a wonderful job raising that man. I loved him so much," she said, reaching across the table to grab Robert's shaking hand. They sat staring at each other until Robert cupped her hand with his free hand and gently shook it, doing his best to smile at her. Seconds passed before he released her hand and got up for more coffee. Robert walked into the kitchen, but turned to Annie when they both heard footsteps on the deck approaching the door. She gave him a funny look and stood up to greet the visitor.

There was a gentle tap at the door just before Annie opened it. A friendly face smiled at her. Pausing, she tilted her head and said, "Hello."

The stranger smiled back and rested his sunglasses on his head. "Hello, Annie."

Robert had entered the living room carrying his coffee cup when he made eye contact with the man. The two stood silent for a second, staring at each other. Annie stood aside, watching Robert assess the stranger. Robert gestured for the man to come in. "Hello, boy, how are you?"

"I'm all right, I guess," Junior replied, smiling as his father went back into the living room. Annie offered to take Junior's sports coat. He walked in, gazing at the photos and furniture. Much of it the same as it was 10 years before.

"Would you like a cup of coffee?" Annie asked as she walked toward the kitchen. Junior gestured with a nod as he picked up an old photo of his mother. Robert watched as he looked at the photo, dusting it with his hand, smiling as he studied it. He set down the picture frame and lifted his face to see his father glancing at him. "You look good, Dad."

Shaking his head, Robert bit his lip. "There ain't much good out there right now, boy."

Junior nodded. "Yeah, I know."

Robert sat down and stared at his son, eyes showing both compassion and disgust. "How long you back for, son?" Junior shook his head, smiling as Annie brought him a cup of coffee.

"I don't know. The wife and I are having some troubles. She took the kids for a few weeks to visit their grandparents." Robert leaned back in his chair.

"How old are your kids now?" Junior sipped his coffee and smiled at Annie. She sat down, interested in the conversation, rubbing her free hand along Hank's ears.

"Well now, William is seven and Thomas is five."

Robert smiled and looked at Annie. "See, McDonoughs always have boys."

Annie nodded, shaking her head and looking at Junior.

"Annie's got Billy's boy inside her." Annie sat back in her chair, reacting to the comment. Junior looked Annie over.

"You are pregnant?"

Annie smiled and nodded. "Yeah, just a few weeks."

"So, your boys are doing good?" Robert asked again, shifting the conversation back toward Junior.

"Yeah, they are. Hopefully, me and the wife can work things out. They are too young to realize anything is wrong." Junior looked over at Annie, still puzzled that she was pregnant, and he was struck by sorrow.

"Yeah, Dad, next time you are in New York, you can visit them," Junior said smiling, trying to bring some cheer to his face.

"Yeah right, don't hold your breath," Robert said smiling, grabbing a cigarette and lighting it. Exhaling, he looked his son over. "What do you tell them about me?"

Junior turned his chair, gave his father his full attention and paused, shrugging his shoulders. "I told him that you were sick and that we could not visit you. Liz, my wife, well, she knows the truth, but the kids don't."

Robert bit his lip and looked away. His eyes caught an old photo of his three boys hanging crooked on the wall. Junior watched his eyes and followed them to the photo. They both sat silently, staring at it.

Junior continued, "I have a photo of you and Grandpa standing against an old growth spruce." Junior paused and watched Robert's face. "The kids always show that photo to people when we have company over." Robert's eyes began to tear up as he quickly glanced at Annie, who was crying already.

Robert smiled at Junior. "Are your boys the logging type?"

Junior shook his head. "Wouldn't ever let them near it."

Annie nodded in approval before she got up and whispered, "I need to lie down." Both men nodded at her and watched as she walked slowly toward Billy's room. Closing the door, she leaned against it, glancing around the room at the pictures on the wall and the clothes on the ground. She began to undress, watching as her black dress fell to the ground. She kicked it aside. Leaning over, she grabbed one of Billy's clean shirts and put it on. It draped over her thin frame. She gasped with a sigh, her nose running with sadness. She sat down on the bed and rolled over in a fetal position. Her belly ached as she cupped it with both hands, messaging in gently. Her eyes began to close; her mind began to unwind. The voices in the other room grew to whispers and disappeared as the early evening breeze blew in from the cracked window, curtains blowing in and out.

As the two men continued their conversation, the coffee drinks turned to whiskey. Robert set down the bottle of whiskey between the two. All the years of bitter anger the father had toward Junior had left momentarily. Junior's frustrations and family stubbornness had been left down the road somewhere. The two exchanged stares and words as the evening sun began to lose itself over the ridge.

"I figured you would be one of them sissy martini drinkers," Robert sad as he sipped his whiskey.

"I drink most things that are sitting in front of me."

"You rich?"

"I have some money."

"You sure dress like it. Shit, damn queer like."

Junior smiled at his father. Leaning back in his chair, he glanced around the room and stood up, walking from one photo to the next, examining each photo closely. "I remember this one with Boone."

Robert lifted his head and squinted toward the picture. "Yeah, that's when your mom was yelling at me not to let him swing the maul at the logs."

Junior chuckled. "You and me argued that day too, didn't we?" Robert began to take his shoes off and lifted his head again to study his son.

"You were always questioning me and being a little shit. Hell, you never wanted to do anything except read books and such."

Chris Glode

Junior stared at his father as he set down the photo. He lowered his head and continued to slowly walk around the room. Robert watched for a second before he reached down to take his other shoe off. Reaching over to the bottle, he poured himself another small dose of whiskey. Junior stopped and looked back at his dad. "I guess I just did not want to be you, Dad."

Robert lifted his head and stared at Junior. Nodding, he paused and shot back his glass of whiskey, grimacing a bit as it slowly seeped down to his stomach.

Robert got up and said, "I know you didn't. I understood that, but I did not want to believe it." He walked to his son until he was a few feet from his room. "Listen, it's good to see you, and I wished we had more time, but I got to go run that crew tomorrow." Junior nodded and looked his father over. The old man smiled and turned away.

"What time are we heading out tomorrow?"

"Pardon me?" Robert asked, raising his voice as he turned back toward his son.

"I'm all you got left, Dad, and I can help you out for a bit," Junior said as he set down his glass on the coffee stand.

"Boy, this ain't office work. I don't need your help out there."

"I want to help you out, even for just a few days or a week or two."

Robert shook his head. "All right, boy, be ready to leave at five in the morning. I got some extra gear for you in the shop."

The old man turned around and chuckled as he entered his bedroom. Junior watched his father shut the door. He walked slowly back to the kitchen and listened to the silence. He noticed Hank was following his every move. He walked over and knelt next to him as the dog sighed and welcomed the attention. Getting up, he walked toward his old room and opened the door. A few boxes rested on his old bed, still intact. He set them on a table nearby and lay down fully clothed, resting his arms behind his head, glancing at the window, listening to the wind blow through the brush and tall trees. His eyes shut and his body sank into the bed. It seemed like only a few minutes before his dad kicked in the door. "Let's turn and burn, boy!"

Printed in the United States
137708LV00001B/203/P

9 781598 587746